Amy

MOA

A.M. Holloway

Published by:

Your Book Company

eBook ISBN: 978-1-7359152-0-3

Paper ISBN: 978-1-7359152-1-0

Library of Congress Control Number: 2020918268

Printed in the United States of America.

Chapter 1

In the deep moonless shadows, eight men anxiously await their commander's go-ahead. These men belong to the Specialized Weapons and Tactics team of the FBI. All eight are in their respective positions, ready to move.

James Burke, special agent in charge, glances at the video monitor again for movement inside the house. In his twenty-eight years of service, he's been a team leader for fifteen. You never know what surprises you'll run into during an operation of this nature. Once the last perimeter check occurs, Burke shouts, "Go! Go! Go!"

Burke listens over his earpiece for what seems an eternity. His team of eight responds one at a time with an "all clear, no contact." So in those tiresome two minutes, his blood pumps hard and fast, sweat beading upon his brow from exhaustion. Burke and his team are tracking a serial cop killer in the Virginia area. Someone is killing police officers at an alarming rate, and the FBI is racing to find this killer. Burke gathers his team.

"Someone explain to me what happened!" barks Burke. He does not have failed missions, as his team is one of the most highly trained in the FBI. This team serves the country in a variety of capacities.

Agent Spencer Lawrence steps up and replies, "Not sure, sir. The house was under surveillance for the past twenty-four hours. According to the surveillance teams, the suspect entered his premises at 0400 yesterday. No one saw him leave."

"But he did. So find me a way out of that house undetected! Now the killer is still on the loose!" After taking deep and calculated breaths, he glances back at his men. "Meet me in the conference room at headquarters in one hour for debriefing and an after-action report."

His obsessive nature requires him to document his failures. No one likes serial killers targeting cops. "What a nightmare," he mumbles to himself. As he walks back down the hallway, he contemplates the damage a sniper rifle can inflict on an unsuspecting fellow law enforcement officer. The vision makes him dump his coffee, as he lost his appetite for the rest of the day.

Chapter 2

SAC Burke's career began right out of the service, and he became a legend at the FBI. After decades of service, Burke remains an imposing figure with his broad shoulders, trim waistline, and signature style haircut. Burke continues his physical training because he competes with the younger generation agents daily. Over the years, Burke completed and excelled in all the specialized training offered, from crime scene investigations to blood splatter, hostage rescue, and SWAT. Now he is one of the senior firearm instructors at Quantico and a team leader on the FBI's number one SWAT team.

Nighttime is Burke's favorite time of the day. Sitting in his rocking chair on the back veranda of his home, he enjoys his favorite bourbon. It helps dull the dangers and fears of his job as he analyzes after-action reports. His house sits next to the Prince William National Forest, which gives him, an avid outdoorsman, comfort.

As he raises his glass to his lips, he suddenly senses something amiss. The silence of the forest is a dead giveaway of impending danger. As he gazes toward the forest, he glimpses a flash of light. Burke has a fleeting thought, "Muzzle flash?" His first instinct is to take cover, but the bullet's impact drives him deeper into his rocker. As the bullet tears at 3,200 feet per second through clothing and skin, splintering ribs and rupturing lungs and heart, he feels nothing. The bullet's impact forces blood and air up his throat, causing a mixture of his blood and bourbon to spray across the freshly painted deck. Burke's paralysis doesn't stop his mind from calculating the muzzle's sound. In Burke's dying thoughts, his training kicks in, concluding the sniper is 250 yards away.

Chapter 3

Mackenzie "Mac" Morris enters the FBI office in Atlanta. She is giddy when she puts on her badge every morning, giving it a rub for good luck. Mac and the rest of the crew sit in a conference room on the eighth floor. The office is abuzz this morning, but not with small talk. All the agents and supervisors are in their offices working the phones. Mac and another agent, one she hasn't met yet, glance at one another, and both shrug their shoulders. "At least they don't know what's going on either," she mutters to herself. Mac studies the faces of the people in the room. Her pulse picks up, and her tension increases because she senses something has happened.

Special Agent Williams enters the conference room with his head up and worry lines etched on his forehead. The attendees quiet down when they notice his concern as they expect a statement. As calmly as he can muster, he announces the ruthless killing of one of their own. Someone gunned down Special Agent in Charge Burke last night at his residence next to Prince William National Forest, right outside Quantico. He explains the details of Burke's death by sharing that someone shot him in the chest with a high-powered rifle, and given the distance of the shot, we surmise a sniper pulled the trigger. The CSI team is still on the scene and will update them with any additional details.

Williams continues, "Burke's wife was at home at the time of the shooting, and she heard the shot. He remained in his rocking chair with a chest wound when she found him. She didn't see or hear anyone, as she only heard the shot. She thought the shot came from the woods behind the house. The FBI has a team of agents reviewing Burke's cases, past and present, for potential leads into who might want Burke dead. No one believes this shooting is random, but we must investigate all avenues. I'll update you when I have more information. Questions?"

Mac raises her hand. "One question, sir. Are you referring to SAC James Burke—the firearms instructor at Quantico?"

"Yes, James Burke. Were you familiar with him?"

Mac advises the group that SAC Burke was one of her instructors during her time at the FBI academy. Her fellow new agents agree with Mac. SAC Burke taught them, too.

Agent Williams replies, "I should have realized this group met him at Quantico. Considering recent events, we'll release everyone early today. Work on cases if you can and be here at 0800 tomorrow."

The agents exit the room in a stupor. The ruthless killing of one of your own is hard to accept. Mac stays back in the conference room to come to terms with Burke's death. She stares out the window, seeing nothing, when Spencer Lawrence, Mac's new partner, walks to the doorway and stops.

Mac is gorgeous. Beauty and brains are the most accurate description of his partner. Mac stands about five feet eleven with long, lean legs, and auburn-colored hair reaching midway down her back. Her eyes are the most fantastic color he's ever seen, and he can only equate them to gold-flecked emeralds. He doesn't know how he got so lucky to have Mac as a partner. He wasn't happy when his boss told him he would partner with a rookie, much less a girl. But now they have been partners for two weeks, and they've been the best two weeks of his life.

"What are you thinking about?" Spencer asks Mac.

"SAC Burke."

"Excuse me, did you say SAC Burke?" replies Spencer with a head tilt and his eyebrows together.

"Yes, didn't you get the news? Someone murdered SAC Burke last night at his home when they shot him to death in his backyard. Agent Williams just told us a few minutes ago. That aside, what are you doing here? I thought you were away on an assignment."

Spencer states as he rationalizes the death, "The assignment failed, and I caught the first plane home. My assignment was with SAC Burke. I just saw him late yesterday. Are you sure it was SAC *James* Burke?"

"Yes, I'm sure. I asked Agent Williams myself." Mac keeps her gaze away from Spencer. She doesn't want to show weakness by shedding tears. Mac isn't one to cry. She grew up with two older brothers, and they taught her not to show any vulnerability. Mac continues, "Agent Burke and I hit it off when I attended his class. He told me he lost a daughter in a traffic accident involving a DUI driver and that I reminded him of her. I guess I just had a soft spot for him. I can't believe he's dead."

Spencer shakes his head. He can't believe Burke is dead either. Less than twenty-four hours ago, he stood beside the man, working an entry with him. What happened to Burke? Spencer suggests to Mac, "Why don't we grab a cup of coffee? You like those frilly drinks, and they seem to calm nerves. Agent Williams will contact us when he receives an update from the team. We have pending cases that require our attention."

"OK," Mac says. "A skinny latte is in order."

Mac and Spencer make their way around the corner of the office to the nearest coffee bar. When they enter, there are several agents already sitting at a table. Spencer introduces Mac to the agents. He isn't sure whom she's met, but he doesn't want her to feel left out. Mac shakes hands with Drake, Cameron, and Justin. The guys have been with the FBI for years, and it's obvious Drake is the oldest of the bunch, with the graying at the temples being a giveaway. Mac notices the intensity of his dark eyes, but Drake doesn't talk much. They chat about SAC Burke and try to reason with his death. Drake was the only agent at the table Burke had not trained at Quantico. However, he had worked with him on several assignments.

Mac and Spencer spend a little more time with their coffee and then stroll back to the office to work on old cases. There's a team already in place to investigate Burke's murder. So Mac and Spencer must move forward, even though they want to find Burke's killer themselves.

The following week flies by, with Mac still learning her way around the FBI. Mac and Spencer close more cases. With their workload lighter, they have a late dinner to celebrate. They choose a local steak house. They devour their food, and then, after two hours of conversation, they go their separate ways, fantasizing about the other and neither one wanting to leave.

Early Monday morning, while waiting for the meeting to begin, Mac and Spencer share updates about their respective weekends. Agent Williams enters the conference room wearing the same daunting expression as when he notified them of SAC Burke's murder. Mac becomes still as she prepares herself for the dreadful news. Out of the corner of his eye, Spencer senses the change in Mac.

The meeting begins with sad words from Agent Williams, "We lost another FBI member. Someone gunned down Agent Winston Cummings this morning in his Arkansas driveway with a 223 caliber rifle."

Spencer glances at Mac, whose face turns pale. Spencer reaches over and touches her arm. His touch penetrates the thin fabric of her jacket, but she can't bring herself to face him. Mac tries to follow Agent Williams's words during the brief meeting, but her mind is on Agent Cummings.

Once the meeting concludes, Mac asks, "Spencer, what is going on? Two agents shot and killed in two weeks?" Mac shakes her head to clear it.

"I can't answer. We need to check if any recent information has come in on Agent Burke. Someone shot him with a 223 rifle too." Spencer stops talking as he watches Mac. He adds, "Are you okay?"

Mac answers, "Agent Cummings was in my graduating class. His wife, Laura, must be distraught. They had so many plans. The couple was planning for a family since he graduated, and they were in talks to buy their first home. Now Laura is planning a funeral. He hasn't had time to make anyone mad yet. This makes no sense."

Spencer listens, because she has to get this off her chest. He hadn't realized Winston graduated with her. He should have put two and two together during the morning briefing.

Over the next hour, Spencer and Mac talk with Agent Williams. He adds nothing new about Winston or Burke.

All they have so far is Winston suffered a fatal gunshot wound to the left side of his head from a high-powered rifle. The round lodged in his brain. So they saved a slug for evidence. Special Agent Williams hadn't learned the caliber size yet from the crime scene guys, but it had the characteristics and ballistics of a 223. They canvassed the neighborhood with little results. Two people heard the shot, which sounded from a far distance. The neighborhood sits at the base of a mountain, and one witness suggested the crime scene guys check out the area.

Special Agent Williams whispers to Spencer and Mac, "I'm sharing this information only with you two. This info hasn't hit the streets yet. Mac, I realize you have a personal connection with Winston as you were in the same class at Quantico. I commit to you we'll find whoever did this."

Mac declared with eyes blazing, "I know we will find the killer." She stands and turns toward the door. "Even if I have to do it myself," she mutters to herself as she exits Agent Williams's office. Then Mac leaves the office building with Spencer in her wake. Spencer follows her to the coffee shop. Mac always thinks best at the coffee bar, whether holding a large coffee or a double-shot cappuccino. They walk in silence as they work through their thoughts. They retrieve their drink choices and find a quiet table.

"Spencer, you may or may not be with me on this one, and that's fine. I want you to know where I stand. If no one tracks this killer or killers down, I will handle it on my time. Winston and Burke should not have died like that." Mac shakes her head as she tries to reason out the deaths of two agents. She wonders if their deaths connect somehow and if the killer is the same person killing police officers in Virginia. No one has mentioned that case since Agent

Burke's death. Mac chastises herself for not asking Agent Williams about the Virginia case.

With a pause before replying, Spencer answers, "Mac, I understand your position, and I'll help you in any way I can. I don't want you going off half-cocked on a wild goose chase. Besides, it's a long trek to Arkansas. Let's stay here in Atlanta and see what the crime scene techs tell us. The first order of business is to determine if we have one or two killers—no one mentioned the relation. Next, we have our caseload. I'll use my contacts to get you the information as it comes in, unless Agent Williams shares it with us. Agreed?"

Mac agrees with Spencer while she contemplates the possibility of two shooters. Are these murders related? What are the odds if they are not?

Mac and Spencer catch up on paperwork over the next few days. Mac is grateful for Spencer, as she never imagined having a partner like him. They hit it off right away. If they were not partners, she was sure their relationship would be on a different level. Or, at least, she hopes things would be different for them. Mac would like the opportunity to date Spencer and see where things would lead them. They have a lot in common. She loves spending time with him, even at work.

When her pen lands on the floor, she catches herself staring at Spencer. He's eight years older than her. At six feet five, his physique is more like a brick wall with broad shoulders, not much of a neck, and dark wavy hair to go with his ice-blue eyes. Not the *GQ* look, but handsome in his own right. Ruggedly handsome, as Mama says. Mac stammers, all the while telling herself she shouldn't be thinking about Spencer like that. She just met him, after all, and they work together. Mama also advises keeping work life and personal life separate. It can make life messy and rarely works in anyone's favor. Are we the exception? "Yeah, right," Mac whispers to herself as she shakes the thoughts from her head and grabs her pen to finish out the last file.

With today being Friday, they escape the office early. Mac wants to introduce Spencer to her family, and today is her chance. Mac is close to her family, so it only fits that they meet her partner. They drive for almost an hour to an Atlanta suburb and turn onto a long driveway where trees line both sides. When they come upon a clearing, there sits the most magnificent home Spencer has ever seen. The house is custom built with rustic and new craftsman features combined in a modern way. This combination of brick and logs makes for an impressive homey facade. The home boasts a huge front porch framed by enormous log columns and massive picture windows. Mac takes Spencer in the side door since friends and family never use the front door. Mac's mother, Mary, greets them as soon as they enter the kitchen.

"Welcome!" Mary opens her arms as an invitation. Mary is happy to visit with her daughter, and the happiness radiates in her eyes. Mac steps up to her mother and kisses her on her cheek. Mac introduces Spencer, and in the same breath, asks about her dad.

"He'll be in soon. He's out back with the kids." Mac grins and asks Spencer to follow her as his eyes grow wide and his upper lip beads with sweat.

He quietly whispers to Mac, "Kids?"

Mac giggles as she nods her head toward the back door.

13

They step outside into a grand backyard and watch Mac's dad, Myles, play with Bullet, Radar and Magnum. Each dog is a rescue of one breed or another, and they love their bone-shaped swimming pool, which sits next to the kidney-shaped human pool. It's hard to keep them out of it sometimes. Dogs are an enormous part of her life and always have been. They were her playmates when her brothers weren't around and her students when she wanted to be a teacher. Mac glances at Spencer as relief floods his face.

Spencer exclaims, "I was a little nervous I was missing something about you!" He takes his hand and wipes the sweat from his face. It's not that he dislikes kids, but he isn't sure he's ready for them. First, he needs to find a wife and one that understands his work life. His work entails many late days and days away from home.

"No kids for me and only a few ex-lovers. Just in case you were wondering." Mac winks.

Introductions, licking, hand and paw shaking continue for several minutes. Finally, the dogs, along with their humans, enter the house together. After Myles escorts the dogs to their room for supper, he joins everyone at the table. They seem to enjoy each other's company.

Myles brings up the subject of Agent Cummings. Mac and Spencer take turns sharing what information they've learned. Mac already told Spencer her dad is a retired military man with deep connections in black ops—marines, to be exact—and Myles has the medals to prove it. He now owns and operates a private investigation firm, I^2, and it spans all four corners of the country. This firm is not typical because it handles many cases and causes for well-to-do people from all over the country. Throughout the meal, Myles questions the duo about the case regarding the lead investigator and if they have viable leads. Mac shakes her head no.

"Dad, I've never been as shocked as when I heard the news about Winston. We were shooting and training partners. I can't imagine why someone would want him dead. Winston was involved in nothing big for the FBI yet. He was just learning the ropes like me."
Myles talks through various scenarios, beginning with feuds in his sphere of influence, drugs, family issues, and prior work experience. Then he circles back to Burke's murder. They lean toward the latter. If revenge isn't the motive, it must be someone close to him because they knew when he left for work.

Speaking in his matter-of-fact way, Myles stated, "I want you both to watch your backs and each other. The way this happened doesn't sound right to me. I predict there will be other killings." They finish the meal with Myles's last thought rattling through their minds. After they exchange solemn pleasantries and clear the dessert dishes, the evening comes to a somber end.

Mac's mood is bright this morning. Work has been productive now that she's more comfortable in her office at the Atlanta FBI headquarters except for a nagging sensation of being watched. However, she finds no one suspicious. She gets along well with her new partner, Spencer, and they spend the better part of the week working on cybercrimes. Mac learns a lot about the computer end of the underworld. She helps propel an investigation by sharing recent computer information in *drafting*. Her coworker is a tenured agent unfamiliar with this term. So she explains how people set up email accounts and then write drafts, never sending actual emails. They save the drafts in the draft folder, and the person they are working with logs into the same email account and then repeats the process. They can read the latest draft and then enter one as a reply. Mac's knowledge of drafting helps the cyber guys crack a car theft ring that had been working in south Atlanta for about six months. This ring was closing in on stealing approximately one hundred cars and chopping them up for parts. With Mac's help, they busted the auto theft ring with thirty arrests in two states.

As Mac finishes the paperwork on the auto theft ring, Spencer, sullen and withdrawn, walks into the office. Mac senses something is wrong. His blue eyes tell the tale because they turn deep blue when trouble calls. The eyes always give it away.

"We have another murder. It appears your dad was right. These are not just random shootings." Spencer's brow bunches as his eyes turn downward.

Mac stares at him, and a few heartbeats later, she groans, "Another killing. Tell me everything."

"The murder took place in Orlando this time. Someone shot Mason James in the head as he drove out of his driveway this morning on his way to work. I don't like this at all. He's another new agent. Tell me Mason wasn't in your graduating class."

"Wish I could," states Mac. "He was a smart guy, almost nerdy. I figured he would go far in this industry. He had the brains and the looks." Mac tells Spencer that Mason lived close to Disney World, and the class teased him about living in fairy-tale land. His first job was dressing up as the character Mickey Mouse. Mac's eyes water as she recalls memories about Mason, the big, overgrown goofball. Then she regains her composure and stops sharing.

Sometimes Spencer wishes she would let go of her emotions. Keeping your emotions all pent up isn't good for the soul. He felt Mac should open up to him because their relationship was growing. This situation was an opportunity for him to show his concern for her well-being. Besides, Mac should share her thoughts with him. After all, they are partners.

Minutes later, Mac is all business. The time to get serious about this investigation is now. She doesn't know how to get involved in the official investigation, but she would find out. Spencer asks her if she wants to contact Special Agent Williams.

"Yes, we need to start with him, given that we have no other contact. Who are the lead agents on the investigation?" Mac questions.

Spencer replies, "The lead agent is Joseph Stubin. He's from Quantico, but they assigned him to Atlanta recently. He's a thirty-year agent with a great reputation as one who never backs down from a challenge. Atlanta is assigning Brett Baxter, another longtime agent, to the case too."

Spencer guides Mac by the elbow out to the elevator. They stand in silence until the elevator arrives. The ride down two floors seems an eternity for Mac. She cannot get Mason's grin off of her mind.

"I have to do something, Spencer. I can't just sit around and let my classmates get shot. This makes little sense. Is the entire class a target?" Mac frets in a grieved tone while rubbing her temple.

"It's possible the class is a target. If so, you'll hear soon enough. The higher-ups will contact all graduates. They may ask you to go to a safe house until we catch the suspect."

"Work with me on this, Spencer," Mac states. "The latest murders were in unique parts of the country with nothing to tie the victims together but the FBI. The FBI appears to be the common link. To my knowledge, the FBI graduation list isn't public. Are these two deaths and Burke's murder related?"

Spencer's eyebrows scrunch together as he asks, "What are you saying, Mac? Are you insinuating this could be an inside job?" He shakes his head as he considers her question again.

"I'm not sure what I'm saying. However, I know two of my fellow graduates are dead in less than sixty days since graduation. What are your observations so far?" Mac rubs her neck while trying to express her concerns.

"I agree the situation is weird, but I don't see anyone in the agency committing these crimes. That is unimaginable," Spencer states, more to himself than anyone. The thought of someone trying to kill Mac sends Spencer reeling. He'll do anything to protect her, including locking her in a closet for safekeeping, but he understands she will not sit back and let someone else handle the situation because that isn't her. Well, he just found her—he is not willing to let her go now.

Chapter 4

As Mac and Spencer approach SAC William's office, the door is ajar, and he's speaking with someone on the phone. They lean against the doorway and listen to his side of the conversation.

"Similarities exist. Someone shot them with a rifle from a distance. One shot was from just under a half-mile away and the other from between two houses in a residential neighborhood. No one saw anything, including the vehicle color or the gunman's description." When Special Agent Williams raises his eyes, he faces Mac and Spencer. He tries to smile when he asks them, "Can I help you two? I know you listened to my conversation. I won't call it eavesdropping this time, but keep it up, and it will be."

Spencer starts before Williams continues with the lecture. "What have you got, Williams? We're getting a little uneasy here trying to figure out what is happening."

Williams raises his hands as if to say, slow down. "We are full steam ahead. No one has claimed to be the killer. We don't know what to think at this point. Our profile team is working on one for us, and Reagan Little should arrive here tomorrow morning for our briefing. She's already begun on the preliminary workup. I wish I had more for you."

Then Williams turns his attention to Mac. "You want to work on this one, and I understand, but you're in danger. At some point, you might be in a safe house or staying with your parents until we get this figured out. Safety is our top priority."

Mac counters, "I don't want to go running home to dad, and I can't sit around waiting. That's not my nature." Mac stands up and runs her fingers through her hair while she turns her back to the men.

Then Spencer speaks. "Any suggestions, Williams? Mac wants to call Special Agent in Charge Stubin and pick his brain as he might have additional information."

"I can handle that for you. Let me call him for you and set up the phone call. Mac, I get this is personal, so at least let me make the introductions," suggests Williams, and then he continues, "SAC Joseph Stubin will be the contact person for the investigation. He's from Quantico but assigned to the Atlanta office. Another Atlanta agent, Agent Baxter, will also join us." Mac nods in agreement as Spencer shared their names earlier, and they say their goodbyes. The duo returns to their desks two floors up to continue working while waiting to hear from the Atlanta agents.

Mac glances at Spencer when they reach their office door and says, "I need a trip to the coffee store. Want to go with me?"

He smiles and follows her out of the building, knowing their destination. Spencer opens the door for her as the strong coffee bean flavor fills the air. They spot one of their own sitting at a table alone. They walk over and acknowledge Drake. He gives them a nod.

Spencer looks at Drake and asks, "Where have you been? I haven't seen you around the office. Usually, you're in the gym working out before your workday begins. I've conquered deadlifts by myself since my favorite spotter hasn't been around."

Drake keeps his eyes down for a second, then raises his head and says, "I've been traveling a little trying to close lingering cases." After shifting back and forth in his seat, Drake bolts, leaving behind a steaming cup of coffee.

"What's with him? I've only spoken to him a few times. He's direct and to the point. Does he have a partner?" inquires Mac as she watches Drake walk away.

"I don't remember him ever having one. Not sure anyone wants to work that closely with him. He's a loner for sure. A man of few words."

They watch Drake walk out of the shop and head toward the office, but not before he glances back at the duo. He and Mac make eye contact, and shivers run up her spine.

Once they retrieve their favorite drinks of the day, they sit at a corner table and get down to business. Mac throws questions at Spencer, hoping Agent Stubin can answer. Questions about the caliber of the fatal bullet, the shooter's location, any ID on the shooter or suspects, and any possible vehicle involved. They want to know everything. Unfortunately, they will not get all the answers because they're not privy to all the information, just what the agent can share.

Mac and Spencer arrive at work the following day, with Special Agent Williams standing at their desks requesting their presence in his office. When all three are behind closed doors, he informs them about the newly formed task force designed to apprehend the FBI agents' killer. Mac's heart beat rapidly, hoping she could be a part of the task force. When Williams finishes his request, he asks Mac and Spencer if they would take part. Mac about jumps out of her chair while trying to say yes. Williams shares a glance with Spencer as he nods in agreement, too.

"Good, I'm glad that's settled," states Williams. "Spencer," he continues, "the executives reluctantly allowed you both to take part. They want Mac tucked away someplace safe. So with that being said, you must watch her back."

Special Agent Williams notices Mac wants to speak. He says, "No comment from you, Mac. That's the deal." Mac nods and shrugs her shoulders in agreement. "Oh, by the way, Agent Brett Baxter is on his way here. We called him in from vacation.," adds Agent Williams as Mac and Spencer leave his office. "You can meet him in person and find out what evidence they've discovered so far."

Mac glances at Spencer as they walk back to their desks. "Spencer, sorry you have to babysit me."

Spencer smiles. "I can imagine worse things. Now let's get to work. Hopefully, agent Baxter will meet with us soon." The idea of Mac working on this investigation and being in danger is scary. Spencer vows to himself he will protect her while working on this high-profile case.

Both agents work feverishly throughout the afternoon, trying to clear their desks. Mac takes time making note cards about each of the murders. It helps her put the pieces together. She labels the card with the deceased's name while adding points of interest, such as the cause of death, time of death, weather, caliber. Deep down, she knows there's a common thread, but she just can't see beyond the FBI connection yet. No one kills FBI agents, whether seasoned or new appointments, without reason. The enormous question is if Burke's death connects to the graduation class murders.

At 1600, Mac receives the long-awaited call. The task force is meeting in the Atlanta field office at 0800 the following day.

The task force members gather around the conference table on the eighth floor of the Atlanta field office. Williams introduces Special Agent Joseph Stubin from Quantico and Brett Baxter from the Atlanta office, and then Williams begins with the evidence from the scenes. A little while later, Williams's secretary knocks on the door. He steps out of the meeting to receive a phone call. As soon as he reenters, everyone suspects another murder. The face of Special Agent Williams states the obvious. "We have another dead agent. Paul Mabry. He was an agent in our Knoxville, Tennessee, office. His death is the same as the others. But a witness came forward, stating they saw a small light several streets over. This time, the killer missed the head and struck Paul in the neck. A witness heard two shots instead of one like the others."

Spencer speaks, "It could be the killer had an acute case of nerves. Why else would he miss? We have proof he can hit his target."

Williams glimpses Mac as he advises the group that Paul was also part of the last graduating class. Then Williams bellows, "We have to put an end to this nonsense. Paul is number three of the same class, and Mac graduated with this class. That makes it personal for us. Let's take a five-minute break."

When the group reconvenes, Agent Williams asks the task force members if they know a Knoxville agent. Someone they can call for help on the crime scene.

"Last I heard, Drake was going up there to follow up on a cold case." Spencer offers.

"I'll call him, and if he's still in the area, he can stop by the crime scene," Williams says.

SAC Stubin adds, "We need an agent at the scene pronto. We need pictures and intel. I don't want to wait on the Knoxville detectives."

Williams and Stubin step out to call Drake. Drake nearly jumps out of his skin when his phone rings. He rarely receives calls on his work phone from Williams. He answers on the second ring.
"Drake, Agent Williams here. I need you to go over to Agent Paul Mabry's house at 2435 Sugar Maple, Knoxville. Someone shot and killed him this morning. We want to get a head start on the scene. Gather intel and send it to me ASAP."

Drake pauses. "Uh, okay, sir. I'm leaving Knoxville, but I'll turn around. Text me the address, and I'll forward the info to you as soon as I can."

Williams enters the conference room with a strange look on his face.

"What's up, sir?" asks Mac. "You appear puzzled."

Williams replies, "I just had a strange conversation with Drake. I'm not sure how to take him at times. But at least he's going over to Paul's house for us. Let's get back to our meeting. Baxter, you're next. What do we have so far?"

"The victim, Paul Mabry, took a 223 rifle round to the neck as he was leaving for work. No visible witnesses. However, someone heard two shots."

Mac summarizes the intel. "The killer knows the victims' schedules, he uses a 223 rifle, and the victims are from the same graduating class. Other than that, not much to go on." She leans back and asks aloud, "How would someone know who was in a particular FBI class?"

Drake pulls up to the crime scene thirty minutes after his call from Agent Williams. He flashes his badge to the police captain, and Captain Graham walks him through the scene. The captain points out Paul's body sits in a prone position next to his vehicle with a bullet wound to the neck. He bled out in his driveway.

"The ballistics are still being worked at the scene," Captain Graham explains. "The medical examiner is on his way to pick up the body. I hope fragments remain in the victim. Since there was so much blood and shredded flesh, we can't tell if the shot went through and through. We are still looking for a bullet, just in case. We need the ballistic evidence for solid proof to help link these shootings together if there is a link."

Captain Graham studies Drake while Drake stares down at Paul. Graham reaches out and touches Drake's arm, and he jumps slightly.

"Sorry. I didn't mean to startle you, but you appeared to be deep in thought. I need you back here," Captain Graham shares.

"Yeah, I'm trying to process the information." Drake's eyes shift around the area, trying to spot anything of interest.

Captain Graham counters, "I bet all of you Feds feel like targets. Well, take a few pictures for your boss. We also have a witness."

Drake stammers, "Witness? What witness? Agent Williams said nothing about a witness."
Graham explains the neighbor heard the shots and saw a flash of light. Then he says, "We have a team searching for a casing."

"Where?" Drake turned his head, searching the surrounding area.

"Across the street. This is the first shooting with a witness account. I'm hoping this will be our break. Although it doesn't sound like he has too much information to offer us."

Drake stares as they load Paul into the ambulance. Captain Graham breaks his silence and asks,
"If this is too much to handle, leave. I'll call your boss and explain it to him. I'll send copies of our reports and evidence as we gather more today. When we lose one of our own, it touches us all."

Shaking his head, Drake looks at Graham, "I can handle it. I'll start with photos of the car and Paul's location. Who has the witness's contact information? Just in case our guys want to speak with him?"

"I'll get the name for you while you take pictures." Graham walks off, looking over his shoulder at Drake. He shakes his head. There's something off about him, thought Graham.

Graham retrieves the witness's name and spies Drake across the street as he studies the crime scene from a fresh angle. Drake snaps a few pictures and walks back to the car with Captain Graham. He hands Drake a slip of paper with the witness's name and number. Drake thanks the captain for his time and hastily retreats.

Agent Williams sits at his desk when Drake phones. He mentions the photos are on the way, then he adds, "I'm not sure how much this will help. There are no casings or bullet fragments in the driveway, so the medical examiner is looking for fragments in his exam. Someone shot Paul in the neck, and he bled out in his driveway. They couldn't tell if the shot was a through and through because of the damage."

Agent Williams listens as Drake speaks while trying to pick up any additional information. Nothing. It will disappoint the task force. They want to end this rampage because they are nervous. Everyone worries because they fear for the lives of the remaining agents. When Drake finishes his synopsis, Agent Williams sighs.

He tells Drake, "I wanted something new. A fresh lead with a new area of focus. The task force waits for an update. Thanks for going by the scene." While still on the phone, his computer beeps, alerting him that a new message has arrived. Agent Williams ends the call with, "Email received. See you around, Drake." As Williams sits at his desk, he feels he missed something, but he can't recall the issue.

Williams walks into the conference room and notices Mac and Spencer already there, so he joins them. They are reviewing the trajectory of the first two kills. The duo points out the agents died in their driveways and killed from a distance. Do driveway and distance signify anything?

Mac asks Spencer, "What was the weather on the day of Winston's death?"

Spencer turns to the murder book for the answer. He replies, "It was hot and dry with a slight breeze and sunshine."

"What about Mason's?"

"Hot, dry, sunshine and no breeze," Spencer answers.

Mac raises her eyes to face Williams. "What have you got, Williams?" asks Mac. "What is the weather in Knoxville today? No, wait. Let me guess. It's hot, dry, sunshine, and little to no breeze."

Agent Williams glances at Mac and replies with a strange expression on his face, "I believe it is hot and dry. Why are you asking?"

Mac explains, "The first two kills occurred during hot, dry days with little to no wind. Maybe the shooter can shoot distances but can't compensate for wind velocity."

Spencer adds, "If the shooter is in law enforcement, surely they can. It's part of our training. It's ingrained in us. Besides, nowadays, instructors pass out handy pocket cards to help with scope settings. Back in my day, you had to use your brain to figure out your scope settings."

Williams advises, "Here's the story. Paul was leaving for work. He stopped, got out of the car, and placed mail in the mailbox. As Paul reached for the door handle, someone shot him in the neck. A guess is the shot was through and through, but the medical examiner will confirm. He bled out in the driveway."

Mac asks if there were any fragments found. Agent Williams shakes his head no. "Let me go over Paul's shooting. The bullet hit Paul in the neck because he leaned over to open the car door. But if he had remained upright, the bullet's path would have been in the lower head area. I think the shooter has difficulty with math. He can't decipher MOA. His minute of angle calculation was off by one click if he intended to hit his head."

"We need to hold on to that information, Mac. Note it. It might become invaluable," Spencer offers.

Agent Williams adds. "We're getting another member of our team. Her name is Lacey Johnson, and she's from our Tennessee office. She'll arrive tomorrow. Are you acquainted with her? She has been around the agency for a few years."

Neither have met Agent Johnson but are grateful for any help. Williams leaves the room to gather his thoughts before he meets with his boss. Mac and Spencer, sitting at their desks, glance at each other. Both are at a loss for words. Spencer's mind wanders toward Mac, and he wants to ask her if they had met under different circumstances, would she date him? He's having a hard time concentrating when he's around her. His lack of concentration might mean life or death with this killer on the loose. This crazy killing stuff is making it worse. He doesn't want to take his eyes off of her with her tall, lean frame, those gorgeous green eyes, and the hair. He loves her smell in the mornings when they sit next to each other in the task force meetings, the way she talks, walks—wow, he has to stop. These thoughts make it hard on him. He needs to work out and burn off energy. They've been in the room for hours, and his head hurts from staring out the same windows. Since his workday ends with time to spare, he will head to the gym.

Spencer speaks first. "I'm going to work off some energy in the gym. Would you care to join me?" He stands and stretches, waiting for an answer.

"Not right now," answers Mac. "You go on, and I'll catch up with you later." Mac takes a seat at the massive mahogany conference table, giving her clear sight to the murder board. She prays for a fresh revelation as she reviews the information. All three victims were male and graduated from the same class.

Furthermore, while leaving for work, someone shot them in their driveways from a long distance. The weather was the same for all three kills. Mac makes a note to herself to add the weather at Paul's death to the board. They must find this killer quick. Her life might depend on it.

Mac moves on to the crime scene info because she likes to keep it fresh in her mind. She notices something this time. All the victims were alone in their vehicles. She'll mention it in the morning just in case it matters. As Mac stands to leave, she turns to the door and is face to face with Drake. She inhales sharply. Drake's dark eyes are not staring at her but through her. He sidesteps out of the doorway, and Mac all but races out of the conference room. Drake watches as she exits, and a slight grin graces the corners of his mouth.

Chapter 5

As soon as Mac clears the conference room, she takes a deep breath. She can't explain her reaction to Drake, but he unnerves her. She's never felt intimidated by another person before, and she's unsure how to deal with it. Mac tells herself that Drake is just another agent, and she shouldn't fear him.

She walks over to the gym to find Spencer, not realizing the sun has set. Mac trots across the dimly lit parking lot over to the next building. The sound of snapping twigs and crunching leaves catches her attention. She turns around but sees nothing, not even a shadow. She doesn't find anyone in the lot at all. Typically, there is activity. Mac is almost at the door when she drops her key card on the ground. "Great," she mutters to herself. As Mac bends over to retrieve her card, she hears the same sound again, and this time the sound is louder, and louder means closer. The hair on her neck stands up as she draws her weapon and holds it down by her thigh as she enters the building. She takes one more glance back toward the lot. As she holsters her gun, she lifts her eyes and stares at Drake, standing by the gym door.

Drake asks, "Hey, are you okay? It looks like you've seen a ghost."

Mac stammers, "Yeah, fine. How did you get here so fast?"

"I came in through the side door. I'm here for Spencer. Where is he?"

"He's supposed to be in there." Mac points toward the weights area.

Drake and Mac enter the gym together searching for Spencer. Mac thinks it's no wonder there isn't anyone in the parking lot. Everyone is in here. It puzzles Spencer when they come in together since he's aware of Mac's impression of Drake and what he does to her. He also notices Mac's expression.

Spencer places the weights in their holders and asks, a little on edge, "What's up? Not another killing?" He takes a towel from its stand and wipes his face.

Mac answers first, "No changes. I wanted to tell you I'm heading home. And I'll see you in the morning." Mac shifts her feet while speaking with Spencer.

Then Drake adds, "I came by to tell you I emailed photos and the requested intel to Williams. Have you found out anything new about the victims?"

Spencer replies to Drake in a concerned tone while staring at Mac, "Nothing new right now. We have another task force meeting in the morning."

Drake scans the area. Turning back to Spencer, he says, "See you around."

Mac and Spencer exchanged worried glances as Drake exits.
Spencer studies Mac. "OK. What's wrong? Drake said nothing to you to upset you, did he?" He places his hand on her forearm and rubs his thumb back and forth.

"No, but I just had the weirdest thing happen." Mac recounts her trip over to the gym. "I didn't see a solitary soul on my walk over, but someone followed me. I swear it was Drake. How else did he get here before me?"

Spencer pauses. "It might have been Drake, but he didn't purposely scare you. Maybe he didn't realize how bad it spooked you." Spencer's insides tremble with the thought of someone pursuing Mac.

Mac cuts her eyes at Spencer. "I hope you're right. Well, I'm heading home since we have an early meeting in the morning."

Spencer grins at Mac and says, "Not without me. Give me five minutes to get my things, and I'll walk you out. Remember, I'm supposed to keep my eyes on you."

The following day the task force meets with two recent additions. Agent Williams introduces Reagan Little and Lacey Johnson. "Good morning. I want to welcome Reagan and Lacey to the team. Reagan is an FBI profiler, and SAC Lacey Johnson is from Tennessee. We'll start with Reagan."

"Thank you, Agent Williams. I'm glad to help, and I need to apologize for taking so long to meet with you. I've been in California working on a serial killer case which I can report we captured him! So now to get this killer behind bars. Your suspect is male and an avid shooter. He harbors a serious issue with law enforcement, specifically FBI agents. His sights have been on male agents, but keep in mind, that can change because we haven't proven it be males only or just the title FBI agent. The suspect is likely in his early twenties to mid-thirties with an unsettled childhood. There's a major connection to the FBI with the possibility he was a rejected FBI applicant or a former convicted felon. We're exploring these avenues and scenarios."

Baxter and Stubin peek at Mac. They wonder if she'll mention the list of newly appointed agents being unavailable to the public. She doesn't make eye contact with anyone. They speak up and suggest they have considered the killer might be one of them because who else would have a list of newly appointed agents? Mac nods her head in agreement.

Stubin adds, "We don't want to investigate our agents unless we have to, but if one of our own is responsible, we have no problem investigating and charging them with murder."

Reagan asks the group, "Has any of you noticed anyone in your offices acting unusual? Like not showing up for work or not returning calls? If so, let's hear it. These instances can be a warning for something dire." Reagan's head turns as she makes eye contact with the attendees.

Mac peeks at Spencer, and he shakes his head no. Mac lets Spencer decide even though she thinks Spencer should bring up Drake. Her gut tells her something is a little out of whack with him.
"OK." Reagan adds, "I have the ballistic report with me, and I'll make sure you all get a copy. The killer shot each victim with a 223 caliber rifle. The fragments were still intact enough that with the ballistic info, we can match it if we ever find the weapon."

Mac asks Reagan for a picture of the fragment. She reads the report and then studies the fragment for a moment. Then she states, "It has a few striations on it, which leads me to believe they fired the bullet from a Remington Model 700. All weapons are distinct in the number of lands and grooves and the width of said lands and grooves. Another characteristic of any weapon is the striation's direction, which forms as the bullet exits the barrel." Mac states and then acknowledge the report's findings.

The group openly stares at Mac. She surprised them all, even Spencer, with her ballistics knowledge. Mac's love of weapons catches him unaware.

Mac grins and explains, "I like ballistics, and I've studied ballistics for several years. My dad taught me a lot over the years. I've been around guns since I was young. Sorry if I got a little carried away with my explanation." Mac looks at Reagan as she talks.

Baxter asks Mac, "How long have you been an agent?"

Mac turns toward Agent Williams, looking for reassurance of her answer. Williams answers for her. "Mac is new. She's part of the last graduating class, and Mac is aware she's in danger, but she asked to be a part of this task force. In my opinion, she's a ballistics expert. Any information she can tell us on that side, I would take to heart."

Mac, a little embarrassed, gives a slight grin and mouths, "Thanks."

Reagan adds, "I should point out the Remington Model 700 is the weapon of choice for law enforcement, including the FBI. Mac's statements, along with Stubin's and Baxter's comments earlier, confirm we need to rethink our direction and concentrate on someone in law enforcement, including our own."

"Agent Williams, I suggest we begin with Internal Affairs. They can apprise us of any current investigations. That will be a suitable place to start. Keep detailed records so you can inform the rest of us. We'll break for today and start again in the morning," Reagan says as she reviews her notes.

The task force members begin the tedious chore of packing their gear when Reagan remembers something. "Oh, by the way, which one of you spoke to the witness in Paul Mabry's murder?"

All eyes turn to Reagan, and all mouths hang open.

Mac speaks first, "What witness? No one mentioned a witness."

All the task force members agree with Mac. The knowledge of a potential witness and the realization that no one is aware of it jolts Agent Williams's senses. He chastises himself for not following up on the witness. Did Drake deliberately leave the information out, or did he forget?

Reagan states, "Captain Graham from Tennessee said one of Paul's neighbors heard the shots while he was in his yard. He said he saw a circular flash of light. My guess is it must have been the scope reflecting the sun." Reagan glances at Lacey.

"She's correct. A patrol officer spoke with the witness. He gave us a wide area to search for the flash of light he saw. We're still working with local law officials to find where the shot originated. The location is on a mountain about five hundred yards from the kill scene in a wooded area. It will be almost impossible to pinpoint the shooter's perch," Lacey offers.

Stubin suggests someone interview this neighbor by phone. They need to get his description of the murder first hand. It might add nothing to our investigation, but it will be one more witness we can mark off our list.

Agent Williams reminds the group that Lacey will share any recent information on their investigation tomorrow, and we'll adjourn the meeting until then.

Spencer follows Mac, whispering in her ear, "So what else is there about you I need to know? That ballistics stuff back there was impressive."

Mac smiles. "Oh, so you like it. A girl has to have some secrets up her sleeve."

Spencer counters, "Ballistics is an exciting secret. I would never have suspected you as a ballistics expert. However, after meeting your dad, I figured you were capable with firearms."

Mac touches Spencer on the arm, and their eyes lock.

"Thank you."

"For what?" Spencer asks, not understanding her reason for saying thanks in the middle of a discussion centered on ballistics.

"Just for being here with me during this crazy mess. I can't believe I've been an agent for less than ninety days, and we're investigating the murder of fellow agents."

Spencer replies with a devilish grin, "I wouldn't want to be anywhere else."

In his mind, Spencer has her in his arms, kissing her. Her touch sends sparks up his spine. He can't decide if he should share his feelings for her or wait until this investigation is complete. A dinging sound interrupts his thoughts, so he glances at his computer. Agent Williams emailed pictures of the Paul Mabry murder.

They round the desk to get a better view of the screen. Spencer opens the image file on his computer for him and Mac to view. It shows Paul's car at the end of the driveway and the body's outline on the ground beside it. Trees obscure one side of the vehicle, and the front yard is on the opposite side.

Mac asks Spencer, "Wasn't Paul shot in the neck?" She tries to remember the stats of the murder.

"Yes," answers Spencer. Then he continues, "This murder took two shots based on a witness description. So there should be another bullet somewhere around the car." Mac suggests calling Captain Graham and asking him to search the car and the surrounding area for the bullet.

"Sounds like a plan. If not in the car, it might sit in a tree or somewhere in the yard. There appears to be lots of trees and shrubs on the far side of the car."

Mac places the call to Captain Graham and explains their idea on the bullet count. Once the call ends, Mac tells Spencer that the captain will call back if he has something to report. He didn't seem hopeful. Captain Graham said they had already conducted a thorough search of the car and the general area.

Spencer replies, "Why weren't we told about the witness? Didn't Drake go over to the crime scene for pictures? He should have said something."

Mac lifts her eyes, turns to Spencer, and says, "You don't suppose he withheld the information?" She shrugs her shoulders.

Spencer hesitates a second. "I sure hope not." There is nothing Drake will gain by withholding information.

Agent Williams calls Mac and Spencer into his office.

He states rather sternly, "Mac, the FBI director, is asking me to pull you from the investigation for your safety. He wants you to report to a safe house. We have a house set up with seven other agents staying there. So there would be plenty of room for you and you too, Spencer if you chose."

Mac says nothing. But she shakes her head from side to side, not willing to give in yet.

Agent Williams continues, "Based on the other kills, time is not on our side. He may strike again in the next couple of days." His eyes shift from Mac to Spencer as he waits on an answer.

Mac speaks first. "I'll stay in the office. The investigation is here. There's a shower in the gym I can use while I'm here, and delivery restaurants are all around the office."

Instead of the office, Spencer suggests Mac stay with him at his place. Agent Williams, with one eyebrow raised, says, "Are you sure? That's a little unorthodox, even for you. Do you care to explain that offer?"

Spencer blushes. "My place is all on one floor. I secure it with an alarm system that alerts the police. It would be easier to watch after her there versus an apartment building with people coming and going at all hours unless she stays at the office." Spencer exhaled a breath.

Agent Williams smiles. "Well, he recovered nicely, didn't he?" Then he chuckles and says, "I will allow it if Mac agrees. It sounds better than staying here."

Mac and Spencer share a glance. "Yes, that will work for me. I'll need to stop by home and get my things."

Agent Williams glances over at Spencer. "Well, what are you waiting for? Go get her things."

Over the next few hours, the duo stops at Mac's place to pack her things and then lands at Spencer's apartment. Mac confirms Spencer is correct about his apartment being on the first floor and facing the parking lot. There are no places to hide near his home as his space is free of landscaping bushes. His parking space is right outside his apartment. Spencer lets Mac have the bedroom, and he takes the couch. Lucky for them, his apartment has a full bath and a half.
Mac wanders around the apartment, thinking about Spencer. His place is neater than she expected. At work, Spencer's desk is a cluttered mess compared to his home life. He decks out the apartment with a brown leather sofa and oversized chair with a matching ottoman. A large flat-screen TV sits atop a table. He didn't know Mac would stay with him, yet the place was dust-free. His apartment impresses Mac more than she wants to admit.

Spencer treats Mac to a cereal breakfast the following day, and he drives her to the office. Mac daydreams of more days like this as she lays her head back on the headrest.

As they enter the office, Mac and Spencer hear the commotion as soon as the elevator doors open onto the eighth floor of the Atlanta field office. The duo burst into the break room. The TV is on, and the reporter recaps the lead story. Someone shot and wounded FBI Agent Fran Evans of the Birmingham field office this morning while leaving for work. Surprised by the outcome, Mac mouths *wounded* to Spencer. The reporter continues by saying Fran lost a lot of blood but should make a full recovery. An air ambulance took her to the medical center in Birmingham for treatment.

Agent Williams asks Mac if she remembers Fran. He hopes she does because he wants Spencer and Mac to handle the investigation.

Mac says, "Of course. There were only thirty-two students in the class and only a few women. The girls supported each other, and we exchanged contact information. You never know when you might need them for something." Mac adds, "I can't believe she's alive. I'm grateful, but what changed? Did he shoot her in the shoulder on purpose, or did he miss his mark?"
Agents Williams and Stubin suggest to Mac and Spencer, "Why don't you two drive over to Birmingham and interview Fran? I'm sure she'll be more comfortable speaking with a female agent."

Both agree. "Let's go. We can be on the road once we grab our things."

Agent Williams speaks to the crowd. "Reagan and I discussed the suspect. Since the killer is no longer just targeting male agents, we're shifting our search to include any FBI agent. We originally thought the cop killer murdered agent Burke as revenge, but now it appears that is not so. Our team added Burke's murder to this case now. Meeting adjourned."

"We'll check in with you as soon as we speak with Fran. Has there been an arrest in the cop killer case in Virginia?" Mac asks, curious about the results.

Williams replies, "Yes, there has been. The Virginia SAC notified me today of the arrest. The cop killer and Burke's death are unrelated. Get going, you two. I hope the suspect doesn't go after Fran to finish the deed at the hospital. I'll reach out to the Birmingham field office just to be sure."

While Spencer drives, he works through potential scenarios. He contemplates an agent targeting other agents, and it makes little sense to him. What is the reason behind it? They ride in silence for an hour. Mac's patience ends.

"Okay," Mac starts. "What plans are you working through now?"

Spencer looks at Mac with an eyebrow raised. "Are you sure you want to hear them?"

"Yes," Mac says as she glances his way. Mac notices Spencer's eyes are a deep blue. The real sign of trouble.

"We have a problem. I'm wondering who we can trust. If this killer is one of us, how can we ID him? If we need backup in Alabama, I'm unsure who to call." Spencer stares at the road as he doesn't want Mac more upset.

Mac stares at Spencer. Because she was so eager to visit Fran, she hadn't considered a backup plan. Mac replies, "I didn't think about that issue because I was too excited to be doing something useful. I'm sorry I keep putting you in this position." Mac ponders the issue too. Since the murders occurred in different areas of the country, the killer could be anybody and anywhere—a fact she is not willing to state out loud yet.

"As I've said before, I wouldn't want to be anywhere else. We'll have to stay close. I kind of like that part." Spencer grins in his devilish way.

Mac watches the sparkles return to his eyes. Her insides burn down deep, and she blushes. How is it possible to have such powerful feelings for someone she just recently met?

Chapter 6

Fifty-five minutes later, Mac and Spencer pulled up to the medical center in Birmingham. They enter the hospital at a trot. Mac approaches the info desk first, flashes her badge, and asks for the room number for Fran Evans.

The pink lady replies, "She's still in ICU under heavy guard. You can find the ICU on the third floor. Follow the blue-colored lines on the wall and the floor."

Spencer takes Mac by her elbow and leads her down the hallway. Mac glances down at the touch. She likes Spencer's hand on her elbow, and she didn't realize how much until now. After multiple hallways and elevator rides, Mac, and Spencer badge their way into ICU to meet with the head nurse. She reports Fran was shot in the left shoulder, right under the collarbone. The bullet went through and through, and it caused a lot of muscle tearing and blood loss, but Fran should recover with physical therapy. She remains under anesthesia from surgery. The nurse requested Mac and Spencer come back in an hour or two, and she showed them the ICU waiting room.

Spencer takes Mac's elbow once again and ushers her out of the ICU. Spencer states, "I didn't see any guards in the ICU or at the door. Did you?"

"No, I didn't. The pink lady said there were guards with Fran."

"Let's stop at the information desk and ask her again," Spencer suggests.

Spencer and Mac return to the desk and wait until the pink lady finishes with someone. Once she becomes available, Spencer greets her and questions her about the guards.

He asks, "How many guards were there?"

She replies, "Just one."

Mac jumps in. "Can you describe him?"

"Sure can. He was nice looking with black hair and dark eyes but not as tall as you." She points to Spencer as she speaks. She continues, "His eyes were as black as I've ever seen. He had a badge, but I didn't get his name nor his agency. I assumed he was local. Did I do anything wrong?"

"No, no." Mac calms her. "We're just trying to locate him."

The pink lady points to the cafeteria, and they take off in a sprint. Mac and Spencer enter slowly, peeking around the door. Only one man sits at a table in the center of the room, and Spencer whispers, "I don't recognize him. So I can't say for sure if he's FBI."

Mac walks over to the table and flips open her badge, and it startles the man. He turns his eyes upward to see Mac's face. Then she asks, "Are you with the FBI? We're meeting an Alabama agent here."

The man shakes his head. "No, ma'am. My son was in a car accident, and I'm waiting for him to get out of surgery." The man twirls his wedding ring.

The duo apologizes for the interruption and leaves the cafeteria. They have the same thought as they run toward the parking lot. The dark-haired man might try to leave the hospital now that they have arrived. No one appears suspicious on the route to the lot.

Spencer states, "He's gone, and I'm hungry. It's time to eat. Let's go across the street to the sandwich shop we passed on the way. We can grab a bite before we go back for Fran."

"Sounds good. I'm hungry too." Mac continues to scan the area.

They exit the parking lot and make an immediate right into the adjoining parking lot. Mac screams for Spencer to stop the car and twists her body to look out the back window.

Spencer slams on the brakes, and he grunts when he presses the pedal to the floor.

"I thought I saw someone familiar. Whoever it was, they looked like Drake. They were passing us going toward the interstate. I couldn't get a tag number. No way for us to catch them now."

"Drake? Are you sure? Should I call him and find out his location?"

Mac pauses, then says, "Isn't it strange he would be here? I'm not even sure it was him. But the driver resembled him. Drake was in Tennessee at the same time as the last kill too. It just strikes me as too much of a coincidence." Mac rubs her temples, trying to make sense of it all.

"You don't like him, do you?" Spencer asks with a furrowed brow.

"I don't know him. Drake hasn't said ten words to me. All he does is stare and grin. I can tell you, Drake spooks me, and I'm not one to scare easily, and he doesn't like to talk with others. It seems you're the only one that claims to be his friend."

Spencer chuckles. "I thought nothing bothered you until the day at the gym. That incident terrified you." The memory of that day floods his mind.

"I can't explain why he bothers me so much. He makes the hair on my neck stand up, and that's never good." Mac reaches up and rubs the back of her neck as she thinks of Drake.

Spencer parks the vehicle and climbs out. "Well, how should I handle Drake? Should I call him and ask for his location?" He looks over the top of the car to Mac for an answer.

"No, don't call. We'll ask him face to face when we get back in Atlanta." After getting lunch, the duo spends time in the waiting room since Fran is still groggy from surgery.

Spencer suggests to Mac, "Let's go over what we have so far."

"Okay. Let me get out the cards." Mac leans over and reaches into her bag.

"Cards? What cards?"

Mac snickers. "It's something else you didn't know about me. I make note cards on all my active cases, including victim information and scenes. Also included on the cards are possible suspect descriptions. It's my idea of a portable murder book."

"Wow! You are full of surprises! Can I read them?"

"Well, I rarely share my cards, let alone show them. But since we are partners and all, I guess it wouldn't hurt to show you." Mac hands the cards to him as a spark of electricity passes through them when their fingertips touch.

Spencer wears his emotions in his eyes. Mac loves those eyes. And the hair. And the body. And the face that comes with it. She might be falling in love with the total package. But she has worked too hard to get where she is by studying and pushing herself to graduate early. She isn't looking to get tied down with a guy. But she sure likes what she sees!

When Spencer realizes what's going through her mind, he takes her hand, and they lock eyes. Each reads the other's mind. Mac rarely blushes, but she can't help herself. Her face turns red every time she is alone with Spencer.

He kisses her on the hand and whispers, "Can I read those cards now?" He asks without losing eye contact.

Mac nods her head yes and hands the cards to Spencer. He takes his time reading each one. He admits the cards are impressive, and Spencer can't get enough of Mac. There isn't anything she does that he doesn't love. He shakes his head. Did he just admit to himself he is falling in love with Mac?

"Wish I had thought of these years ago. they sure would have saved me time."

Mac explains, "When I need the murder book or board, the information is always at my fingertips even if I am not at the office."

"You don't have to explain yourself to me—I like it."

Mac reads the clock. "If Fran doesn't wake up for us to interview her soon, we'll need to stay the night. We'll need a hotel close by the hospital."

"There are plenty to choose from around here. It will be good for us to stay overnight. I'm still in charge of your safety, though, if I remember. I'll take the bed next to the door."

"Who says we're staying in the same room?" Mac asks with her right eyebrow lifted and a grin on her face.

"I do. We're watching our expenses for the bureau, and I can't protect you if you are in another room. If we stay, we're sharing a room." Spencer's tone reflects the seriousness of his words.

"Oh. Now you are pulling rank over me so you can get me to stay in the same room?" Mac asks with a finger pointed his way.

Spencer smirks. "Whatever it takes." Then he shrugs his shoulder. But in reality, with this killer on the loose, he didn't want to lose sight of Mac for a minute.

When a doctor enters the waiting room, he finds Mac and Spencer working on the cards. He states, "Fran is awake but groggy. Her body is weak, so she cannot answer questions tonight. I suggest you both come back first thing in the morning, and I'll make sure your visit is for as long as needed."

Spencer speaks first. "Thanks, Doctor. We appreciate you coming out and giving us the update. We'll return at 0800."

Mac asks the doc, "Has anyone else from the FBI tried to visit Fran?"

"No, but someone calls on the hour to the nurse's station, asking about her condition."

Spencer jumps on the calls. "Are the phone calls recorded, or is there a way to record the conversation?" The excitement is palpable in the room.

The doctor is clueless about the phone system. He calls the head of security and asks him to meet

Mac and Spencer are in the waiting room. Mac is fidgety, so she paces. They are gaining on this maniac, and this could be beneficial.

Ten minutes later, Tim Hall enters the waiting room. He introduces himself, and Spencer explains what they want and why.

Tim answers, "Sure, we can record phone calls on any phone line. Let's go set that up now. Also, I'll assign a plainclothes officer in the ICU to watch over Fran. Since, I don't want the killer coming back to the hospital to finish the job on my watch."

"I like the idea too," states Mac. "We can't afford to lose another agent," she adds as
Tim leads them into the ICU, and they get started. Within fifteen minutes, they have the phone lines set up to record. Now the wait is on.

Mac and Spencer wait a while for the unknown subject to call the ICU again. They wander back to the waiting room and start reviewing the cards when Spencer's cell phone rings. Agent Williams's name appears on his caller ID. Spencer updates Williams on their progress as they wait for the next phone call. Williams confirms the caller is not a task force member nor anyone from the Birmingham office—or at least no one claims to be the caller.

Agent Williams continues, "Agents Stubin, Baxter, and Johnson are interviewing an agent under investigation by Internal Affairs. He threatened several coworkers when we suspended him. Once their interview concludes, they plan to return by noon tomorrow. What are your return expectations?"

Spencer replies, "If everything goes good, we should be home tomorrow afternoon."

"Fine. See you then. Watch your backs," states Williams.

When Spencer looks up, the nurse stands in the doorway. The nurse's station received the call, just like clockwork. Mac calls Tim Hall because they need to hear the caller's voice as soon as possible. Tim responds within minutes, and they follow him to the security office. He pushes a few buttons, and they listen to the conversation. Spencer looks at Mac when the recording starts. The air escapes their lungs when neither Mac nor Spencer recognizes the voice. It sounds male but odd, almost as if it is being disguised. The caller asks the nurse about "Miss Fran Evans's condition," He is polite in his inquiry. As soon as the nurse responds to the caller, the call ends.
Mac asks Tim if there is a caller ID on these phones. "Not typically, but I added it on this phone line when we set up the recording. Let's see what it tells us." He pushes more

buttons and makes a phone call. When his call ends, he is reluctant to address them.

Mac says, "What? What is it?" She can tell Tim doesn't want to give the result.

Tim replies, "The US government registered the phone, and they blocked the number. It doesn't give the actual phone number for safety's sake. And it doesn't tell us which department has the phone in its bank of cell phones." Tim shrugs his shoulders as he knows the information isn't much help.

Neither Mac nor Spencer spoke. Tim admits he can't believe it either.

"Whoever this person is, they are gutsy. They're not worried about getting caught because they know we can't ID them from the phone calls."

"You're right," says Spencer. "The shooter is the caller. Otherwise, why would someone go to the trouble of disguising their voice if they were legit?"

Mac and Spencer thank Tim for his help and make sure the undercover officer is still around for Fran.

They leave the hospital and grab a bite before trying to find a place to stay. Mac picks pizza, and then Spencer says they are getting it to go. They drive around the corner for the pizza and stop at a convenience store for gas. With pizza in hand, they check into a hotel. The hotel furnishings are adequate. As you enter a sitting room, the bedroom is in the back through a door. Mac calms when she inspects the layout and realizes a door separates the rooms with a bathroom in the middle. Spencer instructs Mac to take the bed. He'll take the couch and the front door. She's unsure of her response. No one has watched her back since she moved away from home. Her dad always had her back, along with her brothers. Now maybe Spencer will. She can only hope.

Once they settle, they plop down on the sofa to watch TV. Neither one talks since they are comfortable in the silence. They devour the pizza in record time. With their stomachs full, they talk again.

Mac goes first. "Will we find this guy before he kills all thirty-two of us?"

Spencer's eyes turn dark as he gazes at Mac. "Don't even consider that an option. You're tired and stressed. We both are. Our nerves are on edge, but we will win this battle. And when we do, we can move on to bigger and better things."

Spencer rubs Mac's arm slightly, trying to comfort her. Emotions stir within her, but she doesn't have time for romance yet. It takes all the grit she has to make it day by day with a target on her back. But it's nice to have someone looking out for her.

Mac peeks at Spencer. "You might be right. I am tired. What about a movie? It will help take our minds off of things for a while." Mac questions if anything can take her mind away from the shooter. It's hard walking around in public, wondering if you're the next one with the crosshairs on your back.

Spencer surfs the channels. He finds two movies. One is *Shooter* with Mark Wahlberg, and the other is *Air Force One* with Harrison Ford. She picks *Air Force One*.

Mac clarifies her choice. "I can't watch *Shooter* tonight. It's a little close to home with the killer still on the loose."

"No problem," Spencer replies as he chuckles. "Harrison Ford is a talented actor. He might teach me a new technique or two."

An hour into the movie, Spencer realizes Mac isn't talking anymore. He checks on her, and her head is drooping because she's fast asleep. He slides closer to her on the couch and places her head on his shoulder. The movie could last forever as far as it concerns Spencer. He fingers her soft hair while he listens to her breath. The rhythm of her breathing has sleep overtaking him too.

Spencer nudges her, trying to wake her, but she refuses. So he does the only thing that comes to mind. He picks her up, carries her to bed, and places her on the bed's side opposite the door. After covering her with a blanket, he gets ready to leave the room, but then he glances back at the empty side of the king-size bed. On a whim, he lies down beside Mac, after removing his gun from its holster and placing it on the bedside table.

Hours later, Mac groggily awakens and looks around, trying to determine her location. When it comes back to her, she jumps out of bed, startling Spencer out of deep sleep. He grabs his pistol in the same motion as he stands. Fully clothed, they stand in the bedroom facing each other from opposite sides of the bed.

Mac feels ridiculous, and she bursts out laughing. "I slept so hard. I had no idea where I was when I first awoke! How did I get in bed?"

Spencer replies, "Well, I tried to wake you, but when you refused, I carried you to bed."

"Thank you so much for that, I think. Now time for a shower. What time is it anyway?"

Spencer checks his cell phone. "0615."

"Okay. Good. We'll have time for coffee and breakfast after we dress."

Spencer watches Mac go into the bathroom to shower. The more time they spend together, the deeper his love grows for her. "I can't keep thinking about her like that, but I can't seem to stop myself. I've never felt this way before, and I want to protect her from everyone and everything," Spencer mutters to himself as he shakes his head. He's still trying to sort his feelings for Mac. His brain says one thing but his heart another. He stretches and reaches for the note cards in Mac's briefcase. While thumbing through them, he realizes Stubin hasn't called yet. He needs to remember to check with him later. First, he'll enjoy a leisurely breakfast with Mac, and then they'll interview Fran.

The duo checks out of the hotel and drives to find pancakes for breakfast. The restaurant is located across the street from the hospital. They enjoy coffee, pancakes, and conversation. Not about work, but old-fashioned talking. The conversation steers toward family and childhood. Mac admits her family is close, and they talk all the time. Mac calls home daily to check on her parents. She speaks to her brothers twice a week. Spencer, on the other hand, is far from his family. He's lucky to check in with his mom once a week. As breakfast winds down, it's time to tackle Fran's interview. Both reluctantly stand from the table and head for the door.

Mac and Spencer arrive at a deserted nurses' station at 0800 on the dot. However, relief overwhelms them as Tim, the head of security, approaches them from a side door. Mac's nerves calm when Tim takes them to Fran's room. They moved her overnight to the third floor. She's in a private room with a guard at her door.

Chapter 7

Mac enters the room first with Spencer in her wake. Fran is sitting up with her breakfast tray, sipping coffee. The hospital staff covered her shoulder completely in dressing and taped it down to her body. She is deathly pale, but her blue eyes are bright. She instantly recognizes Mac. Fran places her coffee cup down, and with her uninjured hand, she reaches out to take Mac's hand.

"Mac, it's good to see you. What are you doing here? You should be in a safe house."

Mac responds, "I'm working on this case, and we're here for your interview. First, Fran, let me introduce my partner, Spencer.

"Nice to meet you, Spencer."

Spencer says, "Likewise."

Fran continues, "Well, let's get started. I'm due for pain medicine, and I won't be able to answer anything after I take it. Medications do a number on me."

Mac steps to the left so Spencer can move closer to the bed. Spencer pulls out a small notebook, and the interview begins. "Did you notice anything out of the ordinary over the last few days around your home?"

Fran's eyebrows draw together as she processes the question. "All I remember is a dark-haired man sitting on the hood of a compact sedan a few days ago. He was talking on a cell phone. I passed him twice that day. I thought nothing of it because there are always new people in and out of my street. That's the life of living in a college town. Tuscaloosa is a great place to live, but it's hard keeping track of all your neighbors."

Mac asks the next question. "Could you ID him if you saw him again?"

Fran replies instantly, "I might. I sure would like to try. Is he the shooter? Why is he doing this to us? What is the motivation, and why me?"

Spencer doesn't offer answers to her questions, instead he asks Fran if she'll work with a sketch artist. Fran advises she didn't get a real good close-up look at this guy, but she'll do anything to help catch him. Mac and Spencer thank Fran for her time.

They face the door when Fran yells, "Wait! I just remembered overhearing two officers say the shooter stood between two buildings several streets behind my house when he pulled the trigger. I can't say why he missed me if he was so close. That's all I remember. Thanks, guys, for coming by."

Spencer reaches in his pocket and pulls out his business card. He walks back to her bed and hands it to Fran and tells her to call him if she remembers anything—no matter how small.

As soon as they walk down the hall, Spencer looks at Mac and says, "We have to go to the scene. I want to observe the layout of the two buildings Fran referenced. Maybe the crime scene techs failed to collect all the evidence. You never know. We might get lucky."

Mac agrees, and they head for their vehicle. Once inside, Spencer dials Stubin's number. They are interested to hear if Stubin has found anything on the IA investigation. After five rings, Spencer leaves a voice mail. Mac had hopes of Stubin finding something.

Forty-five minutes later, Mac and Spencer arrive in Tuscaloosa. Mac enjoys cruising college towns. When she was in school, she had an apartment in Athens, Georgia, the home of the University of Georgia. Mac loved the hustle and bustle of a college town during class time and football season. There was nothing like the excitement surrounding a hard-fought college football game on a fall Saturday afternoon. Spencer, on the other hand, curses the traffic. He doesn't know how anyone can live in a town with this much traffic. It takes Mac and Spencer another fifteen minutes to find Fran's house. Once they do, they park in her driveway and survey the surroundings.

Fran lives in a row house. There are four homes per building, with parking for each house in front on a parking pad. She lives in an end unit of the second building. Mac eyes the spot Fran mentioned where the killer might have fired the shot. The shooter moves closer to his targets, which convinces Mac that he can't adjust his scope for MOA. The shooter should have had no problem hitting Fran's head since the land is relatively level from this distance.

"Over here, Spencer." Mac points to a place between the two buildings. "There is a black rub mark on the wood siding."

"What is this? Is it a rubber mark from a gun stock?" Spencer asks.

Mac bends over, inspecting the spot when Spencer yells, "Whoa, boy!"

A big black dog pelts Mac in the back, and she addresses the dog. "Hey, fellow. Where did you come from? You sure are cute." Mac rubs the dog behind the ears while trying to stand.
Spencer cuts his eyes at her and says, "I bet you say that to all the guys."

Mac chuckles as she watches a lady jog over to them. Spencer seems to enjoy watching this lady jog. A grin spreads across Spencer's face as Mac feels the redness come into her own. Is she a little jealous over the way Spencer gawks at this girl? Mac tries to shake it off, but she doesn't remember Spencer looking at her that way. Spencer introduces himself first, then Mac. The dog's owner, Abby Carter, introduces herself and Murray, the dog. She tells them she lives three buildings behind Fran.

Spencer starts with the questions. "Abby, were you here the day before yesterday when someone shot Fran Evans?"

"Yes, I was. I had just started walking Murray when he slipped out of his collar. By the time I got to him, he was over here just about in this same spot. Murry never meets a stranger, so when he spots someone new, he's hard to control until he licks them."

Spencer continues, "Did you notice anyone unfamiliar?"

Abby replies, "The only person I saw was a guy that I didn't recognize. He wore all black, with dark hair and dark eyes. This guy wore a ball cap, and if I am not mistaken, he was the same one I saw sitting on the hood of a car three or four days ago out on the main road over there. After he ran off, tons of police and an ambulance arrived at Fran's." Abby points to the road in front of Fran's house. "I didn't know what happened until afterward."

Mac jumps on this. "Did the guy say anything to you?"

"No, he just trotted away with a big black bag slung over one shoulder and a smile on his face."

Mac asks Abby if she can ID him. "I'm not sure. I only saw him a split second, but I'd like to try."

Spencer steps away from the ladies to make a phone call. Spencer's goal is to find a local sketch artist for Abby, and they need the artist pronto. He hopes Abby hasn't lost the image of this guy. Time is not on their side because the longer it takes to find an artist, the more likely she will lose the vision. He leaves two messages for his FBI contact and then walks back over to the ladies.

"Abby, is there a way for us to contact you later? I left messages for my contact, and once she returns the call, I'll contact you."

"Sure," replies Abby. "My number is on this card." She hands one to Spencer and one to Mac.

Mac and Spencer speak briefly out of earshot from Abby. They figure they have only one question left, and Mac asks it. "Abby, was there anyone else around that might have noticed this same guy?"

Abby thinks for a second and says, "I only remember seeing one car pass by, but I can't recall the driver. The car was a Ford Mustang."

Spencer asks the last question about the car. "Can you tell us the color of the Mustang?"

"Green. Bright green with a black stripe down the center of the hood." Abby responds. "I've seen it over here before, but I'm not sure who drives it."

"Great. Now we need to find this bright green Mustang," states Mac.

"You sure have been an enormous help, Abby. Call us if anything else comes to mind."
Mac and Spencer hand Abby their business cards. Spencer calls back to Abby as they are walking off, "I'll call once we hear from the sketch artist." He lifts his hand and waves as they walk away.

As soon as Mac and Spencer made their way to their vehicle, Spencer called Agent Williams and updated him.

Agent Williams replies, "Fantastic. It sounds like we are making progress. Stay in Tuscaloosa and find this green Mustang. The driver may add something to Abby's description."

Mac tells Spencer they need to find the best bar in town. Someone there will know who drives a bright green Mustang. There can't be too many bright green Mustangs in the area. So they head toward town. Spencer growls under his breath at the traffic. He can never understand why some cities have so much traffic. He absolutely hates wasting time in traffic.

Sitting in the passenger seat, Mac fills out her note cards. Her mind is on these killings and piecing them together. She desperately wants to track down the killer. The family members of the deceased agents need closure. She would wish for closure for her family if she were in their place.

Mac and Spencer spend the better part of the afternoon and evening talking with the locals, but the time proves fruitless. Mac states to Spencer, "People sure are standoffish. They won't even glance our way. Do we look that much like federal agents?"

"Yeah. Dark slacks and white shirts scream FBI. These days, no one wants to get involved. Most people stay in their own little worlds."

Mac has an idea. She says, "I'm coming back to this bar tonight dressed like a local. Take me to the mall. I need extra clothes." She rubs her hands together as her plan comes together.

Spencer just stares at her. "Okay. I hope you know what you're doing."

Mac glances at him as she says, "I've never been undercover before, but I've always wanted to try it." So it's off to the mall to shop for new clothes. As the duo drives to the mall, Spencer monitors the rearview mirror. Mac watches him for a while until she gets nervous.

"What are you looking at, Spencer? And don't tell me you see nothing. You're tense, and your eyes are on the rearview mirror for a reason."

"We might have a tail. There is a dark-colored sedan three cars back in the same lane. They picked us up when we left town for the mall. I can't see the driver because of the traffic. If I change lanes, can you check on the driver?" Spencer asks Mac.

"Yes. Try it. I'm not sure if I can see either, but do it now."

Their car swerves into the next lane between two cars, leaving no room for another one. Mac cranes her neck toward the dark-colored vehicle, but she cannot see the driver.

"Spencer, I can't see the driver either. Drive to the mall. The parking lot will be busy, and we'll track the car."

Several minutes later, they arrive at the mall and park at a major retail store. Spencer finds an empty slot next to the front door. He parks and they exit the car, hoping to spot their tail. The car didn't show. It's as if the car knew their route. Now Mac and Spencer wonder if the killer is following them.

Mac refuses to let the scare of being followed keep her away from the bar. They need to find this green Mustang, and the bar will be the quickest way to accomplish it. Bartenders are notorious for knowing the ins and outs of their towns.

The shopping spree helps Mac settle her nerves. It's a typical outing to try on and choose an outfit for tonight. Once she has it, they grab a bite to eat. Mac and Spencer set the plan for the night and cruise around while watching for the tail before parking.

About 2100, Mac strolls into the local bar, The 8 Ball, with Spencer camped out in the parking lot. "Apparently, 2100 is a popular time," Spencer mutters to himself. The bar is jam-packed with patrons and Mac barely has room to reach the bar. Her auburn-colored hair is curled, her makeup is perfect, and those jeans—Spencer can't believe he let her walk into the bar looking like that! She sure can dress the part. Spencer sees her in the famous FBI attire every day. This is definitely a change and a wonderful one.

Spencer stares through his binoculars when he spots a strapping young man putting his hand on Mac's backside. Spencer laughs because he can read Mac's mind. She wants to deck this guy because she doesn't like being handled. Spencer watches her remove the hand, and then she asks him questions. He reaches for her backside again, and that's a mistake. Mac bends the man's arm behind his back and whispers in his ear. He gives Mac a nasty glare and leaves the building. While at the bar, Mac nurses a ginger ale for what feels like hours. The bartender approaches Mac more and more. Around 2300, the bartender takes a break from making drinks, and he stops by Mac. Spencer continues watching her. He doesn't like her being in there alone. He records the tag numbers of the patrons at the bar, but there are no green Mustangs. The bartender puts his arm around Mac and leads her to a table out of Spencer's sight.

Spencer takes notice of any dark-colored sedans entering the lot. Females dressed for the bar life drive most of them. He jots two tag numbers down in his notes as men exit the driver's seats. Although they don't look like the type of people who commit murder, he still wants to check them out.

He needs his eyes on her, so he makes his way to the entrance. Spencer saunters up to the bar and orders a ginger ale. Once he takes hold of his drink, he swivels his chair around and searches for Mac. Spencer gets nervous when he can't find her anywhere, but he doesn't want to appear eager to anyone. Still, where is she? He checks all the tables and booths in his line of sight. When he doesn't find her, he walks around and surveys the area. She might be sitting in a quiet corner somewhere, so he carries his drink and begins his search.

Spencer is about to give up and call the cavalry when he spots them in the booth next to the back door. He wants Mac to notice him, but he doesn't want to spook the bartender. So, he makes his way to the men's room, down the hall past the booth. Mac faces away from Spencer so she'll see him on his way back into the bar. He walks past the booth and enters the men's room for one minute before exiting. He expects to see Mac sitting in the booth facing him upon his exit. Instead, the booth is empty! What? Where is she now? Wonders Spencer as his head swivels, looking for her. She was just there a minute ago. Now the panic sets in again. Why would she leave the booth? Mac must have seen him walk past. The search begins all over again. He can't find her anywhere in the bar, and there's a new bartender taking orders. Spencer sprints to the car.

When he crosses the street, he spots Mac leaning up against the car with a grin on her face.
Spencer fumes, "Mac, you just gave me a scare. I thought I lost you." He reaches for her hand.
"Please don't do that to me ever again." Still holding her hand, he runs his thumb back and forth across the top of it.

She stammers, "I saw you go to the men's room. I thought you were giving me a signal that my time was up, so I ended the conversation and came out to the car. I didn't mean to scare you."
Spencer inhales deeply. After he gathers his wits, he asks her about the information she collected from the bartender.

Mac states, "The bartender is aware of three bright green Mustangs in this town. All three belong to students, and he'll provide us the names of the kids if I check back with him tomorrow night around 2100."

Spencer's eyes turn dark as he says, "We'll see." Then he turns around, and silently, they climb into the car and head back to the hotel.

The following day, Mac and Spencer update the note cards by adding info gathered from Abby and the bartender. Then Mac peers at Spencer with her eyebrows bunched together.

"What? Is there food on my chin?"

Mac giggles. "No, silly. I'm trying to figure out how our killer and Burke's killer are the same. It might be the same caliber of the bullet, but I wonder if we have two different killers on our hands."

Spencer asks, "What brings you to that conclusion? We haven't received the ballistics back yet on Fran."

"I'm not sure—just a thought. We've arrested no one in Burke's slaying. They shot Burke in the chest. The other shootings have been in the head and neck, except for Fran, which was a mistake because of Murray. Or least, that's my guess why Fran's injury was to her shoulder. We need to ask if everyone agrees that the killer is responsible for Burke too. If not, we have two shooters."
Spencer agrees to speak with Agent Williams and share this new idea.

After breakfast, Mac, and Spencer leave the restaurant when Spencer's cell phone rings. He answers the sketch artist's call and arranges for Abby to meet with the artist this afternoon. He has high hopes Abby can describe the man. If they have a sketch, they can release it to the media to locate this person of interest.

Agent Williams calls Spencer for an update on the investigation. Spencer dives into detail about Abby and the bartender. He doesn't tell Williams about Mac and her undercover work, choosing to keep that information to himself. He doesn't want to get reprimanded and have Williams call him back to Atlanta before they finish the investigation in Alabama. Then Spencer tells Agent Williams about Mac's thoughts regarding Burke's killing. Agent Williams says he'll run the idea by the profiler and the team assigned to Agent Burke's death. Agent Williams advises that the report on the gun cartridge found at Fran's should be back today. Then he asks to speak with Mac.

Spencer passes the phone to Mac. She says, "Good morning, sir."

Agent Williams replies, "Good morning. I just wanted to warn you that IA is investigating all the graduates from the last class. They want to rule out all the graduates and are going back three classes. The profiler is suggesting that the killer is one of us. It will be a while before they get to you. I just wanted you ready."

"Interesting. I'll be ready. Thanks for the warning," answers Mac.

Mac turns to Spencer and repeats Agent Williams's warning.

Spencer asks, "So the profiler surmises the killer is a recent graduate of the FBI academy? That makes little sense. Why would a recent graduate take the life of other new agents? It takes a lot of hard work to make it through the academy. Why give up a chance like being an agent? I don't buy into that theory."

Mac answers with a question. "Have we verified all the people that the FBI let go from the most recent academy?"

"I believe they have. It was my understanding they were going back three classes, just like with the recent graduates."

Mac waits ten seconds. "That's what Agent Williams said too. Maybe that isn't far enough back. This doesn't add up because we're missing a piece." She continues, "Well, let's see what the artist can tell us. When is Fran meeting with her sketch artist?"

"I haven't heard yet. I'm not counting on Fran's sketch to add much. She told us she didn't get a good look at him. We'll still follow up on it, but I'm not holding out much hope."

Several hours later, Abby sits in front of a sketch artist named Sandra. She begins by asking Abby vague questions. She draws on her paper while her questions continue. After an hour, the questions turn more specific. They spend two hours working on each feature, ending with the eyes. Sandra explains the eyes are essential. They must be as close to the actual ones as possible. Then Sandra asks for the hair, and Abby blurts out the hair is short and straight. The front of the hair lies on the forehead. Mac and Spencer share the same sentiment as the letdown is unbelievable. Mac's face gives her emotions away. Abby described Drake to a tee until she reached the hair. Drake parts his hair on the side.

Sandra puts the finishing touches on the sketch and turns it around for Mac and Spencer to view. They stare at it without a reaction because the guy is average. There are no marks or tattoos to identify him. The sketch favors Drake, but it isn't him. The guy in the sketch is too skinny, plus the hair is different.

Spencer asks Abby, "Is this the last one? Is this the guy you saw sitting on the hood of a car outside of Fran's house?"

"Yes. That's him. No question." Abby confirmed.

"Great. Thanks for your help, Abby. You're free to go."

"OK. Let me know if you need anything further." Abby offers.

"We will," replies Spencer as they walk back to their borrowed conference room. Spencer scans the sketch and sends it to Williams. Then he places a call.

Agent Williams answers on the first ring. "Williams," he says into the phone.

"Spencer here. Check your email. I forwarded Abby's sketch to you. Any chance you recognize this man?" While Spencer waited, he tapped his pen against the desk.

Williams says, "Hold on a second." While Spencer waited, the pen continued beating against the desk. Williams groans and speaks to someone in his office. "You are kidding, right? Unbelievable! Here we go again."

Spencer looks over at Mac and shrugs his shoulders. His heart rate jumps. Something else has happened, but he doesn't know who's involved. And he'll have to be the one to tell Mac. He hates seeing the anguish in her eyes. It makes his heart hurt.

Williams comes back on the line. "I have the picture, and the face looks familiar to me, but I don't have a name. Fran's sketch is due at any time. She was working on it, but it was creeping. It will interest us if they match. I am sending it to the lab. They will search for all recruits and graduates. Let's hope for a match. I'll keep you updated. Any new info on the green Mustang?"

"Not yet."

"Well, you need to hurry and find it. We have another shooting. Not sure of the agent's condition. The agent is Zack Shelley. Someone shot him this morning in the driveway of his home."

Spencer stammers, "We're trying for a lead on this Mustang. If not, we're coming home." Their call ends as Spencer tries to contain his boiling emotions before he turns around to face Mac.

Mac speaks first. "What is it, Spencer? I heard part of the conversation. Was there another shooting?"

"Not sure about the agent's condition. The agent is Zack Shelley. The killer shot him in his driveway like the others."

"Oh my. He lives in Anderson, South Carolina if I remember correctly. Spencer, I don't know how much longer I can keep doing this." Mac rubs the back of her neck with her hands.

"Nothing we can do from here to help him. Let's find us a green Mustang. Then we can go home where we belong. Everything we learn is helping get us one step closer to finding this creep. We'll get him. I promise." Spencer reaches over and holds Mac's hand. He wants her to believe him. He will get this guy if it is the last thing he does on earth.

Stubin and Baxter are interviewing dropouts from the last class. Nothing has panned out yet. Those that didn't make the cut have found work in law enforcement in one capacity or another. Most of them landed back at their old jobs or decided on another career path.

Stubin calls Mac. "Hey, can you send me a copy of the sketch?"

"Sure. On its way. I hope you can recognize him."

"I want to show it around headquarters and ask the Quantico instructors if they can put a name to the face." Stubin surmises that if the guy had difficulty shooting with a scope, the instructors would remember him. Even though more people than you think have trouble deciphering minute of angle calculations. Once they determine the trajectory, the bullet drop throws them off. This is because a bullet travels in an arc, and the arc shifts with the wind and other factors.

"Brilliant idea. Keep us updated."

Mac shares Stubin's idea with Spencer, then says, "Wish I had thought of that. Maybe someone will recognize him."

Spencer agrees and goes to the note cards. He adds a few things and declares, "Supper time."
Mac checks her watch. "Great. Let's eat. Then it will be time to meet my favorite bartender!"

Mac nudges Spencer on the arm as she makes her way to the door. Spencer's eyes turn dark as he calms the tingles running up his spine. When this mess is over, he and Mac must talk. He is unsure what Agent Williams's reaction will be when he finds out Spencer loves his partner. But there are married agents at the bureau, and they make their relationships work. So he and Mac should be able to pull it off too. Here he goes talking about marriage when he isn't sure if Mac wants the same. He can only hope. She has no idea what she does to him. Or maybe she does, and she just enjoys watching him squirm.

Chapter 8

At a little before 2100, Mac and Spencer wait in the bar's parking lot. Twinkling stars fill the night sky, making it easy to sit in the car. However, their minds keep wandering back to each other. They have a hard time watching for the bartender. Spencer wants Mac in and out of the bar in a hurry. Mac dressed the part again with black jeans, a sparkly shirt, and cowboy boots. The boots go everywhere. She loves her boots, and Spencer loves her in them. Spencer has a hard time turning his eyes away from her. They are spending way too much time together. He needs to finish this tonight and head back to Atlanta, and he needs space. He enjoys having her totally to himself twenty-four hours a day, but separation must be the answer, or so he thinks. The problem is Spencer can't decide if a break will work for him. He's afraid he's in love.

Mac starts the conversation. "What is on your mind? Your wheels are turning."

Spencer gives her a special grin, and Mac melts. She tells herself she is reading too much into Spencer. Does Spencer grin like that to all the ladies? She doesn't want a letdown when she gets back to Atlanta. That's one reason she doesn't like to get into relationships. They take up too much energy, and she wants to put her energy into her job. But, on the other hand, she knows what she wants out of a man, and Mac never thought she would find it in her FBI partner.

Mac peers out the back window when she spots the bartender heading for the back door, and he isn't alone. He has a young kid in tow, possibly seventeen or eighteen years old. Is this the driver of the Mustang? She hopes it is because she wants to head back to Atlanta. She needs information on Zack's condition. They haven't received an update since that morning, and she isn't sure if he survived.

Spencer advises Mac to enter first and contact the bartender. He's coming along this time and will sit at the bar. He refuses to leave her alone tonight. Another two hours like last night, and his nerves wouldn't be able to handle it.

Mac says, "Okay. I'm exhausted, but we need to get back to Atlanta. Can we stay here one more night and drive home first thing in the morning? I can't keep my eyes open long enough to get home."

"Yes, I agree as I'm beat too. Okay, showtime. You have ten minutes to make contact, then I'm coming inside."

Mac puts her game face on as she exits the car. She glances back at Spencer but says nothing. She just winks. Spencer cringes because he doesn't want her going back inside the bar alone. Spencer sets the timer on his phone. He will not wait any longer than necessary. They never found the dark-colored sedan that followed them on the way to the mall. It niggles Spencer's brain every time Mac walks in a public place.

Once the timer sounds, he enters the bar, which is dark and packed. How weird. It's the middle of the week, and this place is jamming again. The bar must not have a slow night. He spots Mac right off this time, speaking with the bartender and the kid. She waves Spencer over to their table. Then Mac introduces him and tells the kid to talk. The kid turns out to be the bartender's boy. He's eighteen and a student at the college. He was leaving a friend's house when he saw the guy sitting on the hood of a dark-colored car. The kid says it didn't look like a cop car. Just an average four-door compact car and he's unfamiliar with the make or model of the vehicle. The kid didn't get the tag number, either. He says the guy was on the phone, and he didn't see his face because of the way he was leaning on the car. That was all he remembered. He gives Mac his cell phone number in case they have more questions. Mac and Spencer leave the bar disappointed. He takes her hand and holds it on the way to the car.

Mac climbs into the car without speaking as no thoughts come to mind. There are no words to describe how she feels. She has a combination of emotions from frustration to complete and total anger. They spent so much time on this angle with nothing to show. She doesn't risk looking at Spencer because she doesn't want to see the disappointment in his eyes. It makes her even sadder to see Spencer's eyes. She hates to disappoint him.

A few minutes later, Mac speaks, "I wonder if we'll ever find this person or the persons responsible for all this killing." She turns her eyes downward and studies her hands.

"Don't get depressed. Now isn't the time. We're gathering information daily. We'll get this guy because you know we always get the evil guy! Let's find a hotel and get a good night's sleep. We'll leave first thing in the morning and be back in Atlanta before lunch."

Spencer prays he can keep his spirits up to support Mac. She is distraught. He wants to reach across the seat and pull her into his arms. He wants to protect her from the outside world, but that's impossible. She'll experience strange and dangerous predicaments throughout her career. But that doesn't mean he has to like it. Somehow, he has to learn to accept it.

They check into a hotel close to Interstate 20, so they can quickly jump on the highway in the morning and head for home. Silence ensues between the duo because their thoughts consume them. They enter their room and take to their beds. They just lay there and stare upward at the ceiling.

At 0100, Mac rises and walks to the bathroom, where she splashes water on her face. Sleep doesn't come to Mac with Spencer in the bed beside her and a killer on the loose. The investigation aggravates her, and she wants Spencer to hold her. That's all. Just hold her. With her head low and shoulders down, she proceeds back to bed. They didn't even check in with Williams that night. With nothing to add to the investigation, neither one wanted to call him. Mac still doesn't know if Zack Shelley survived. Depression causes a myriad of emotions, and all these emotions make her crazy. Since joining the FBI, Mac has already experienced so much death. She considers working for her dad at I^2. He would teach her the ins and outs of the private investigation world. He's expressed his intention to take over the business one day, but she made her way first by working for the FBI. She dreamed of being an FBI agent since she was a young girl, but she wouldn't have to deal with all this death if she were a private investigator. She would call him in the morning to see if he had any recent information. Myles was working on her case from his side because of her involvement. Her brothers were mad at her because she didn't go to the safe house. Things are not looking so hot in her professional life or her personal life right now. She wanders back toward her bed, and as she reaches for the blanket, someone grabs her arm. She lets out a haymaker and catches Spencer on the right side of his head as she shrieks.

Spencer falls back on the bed, holding his head. "Why did you swing at me?"

Mac reaches for him in the dark and finds nothing. Her fingers land on the light switch, and she bathes the room in light.

"Why did you grab me like that? You scared me to death! I had no idea you were awake. You should have said something," Mac states in an apologetic tone.

Spencer chuckles and says, "Who else were you expecting? Do you think I would let someone come in here and grab your arm?"

"I guess not. I wasn't paying attention, and I'm sorry I hit you. Let me check your head. Is it swelling?" Mac reaches over to look at the damage.

"Nah, I don't think so. I knew it was coming, so I ducked when I saw you swing around." Spencer rubs the side of this head. He's thankful he doesn't have a black eye because he'd have a lot of explaining.

"Right. You saw it coming," says Mac as she turns her head away from Spencer, laughing. She doesn't want to hurt his feelings any more than she already has.

Once they settle back down, Spencer asks Mac to lie with him. He sees the brief glint of surprise in Mac's eyes. He just wants to talk and hold her. She's grateful for this man. As they lie side by side, Mac rests her head on Spencer's shoulder. Spencer wraps his arm around her. He turns his eyes down and comments, "We sure fit well together." Spencer presses a gentle kiss to her forehead, and then he asks her what she was thinking about when she clobbered him.

Mac hesitates and then confesses, "I'm considering working for my dad at I². I have already seen so much death in my first couple of months with the FBI. I never dreamed it would be like this."

Spencer jumps on her reply, trying to persuade her to remain an FBI agent. "Our job is not always like this. There is death, and you knew that. This bit about agents getting killed isn't normal. I've been around for ten years and have experienced nothing like this. Don't give up now. I've said this before, but we're just getting started! We have many years and many cases to work together if you keep me as a partner."

Mac sighs and agrees she likes the sound of that. Spencer hugs her tight, and he suggests she get some sleep. Spencer holds Mac all night.

They wake at 0545 in the position they dozed off — in each other's arms. Their eyes make contact, both wanting to kiss the other and both knowing they shouldn't. The attraction they have for each other is apparent, and it's growing. Mac moves away first and heads for the shower. She is in and out in thirty minutes. She graciously lets Spencer have a bit of scalding water this time. While Spencer dresses, Mac uses her time alone wisely. She works on her note cards, trying to take her mind off of Spencer, which isn't easy these days. She adds details about her conversation with the boy and the green Mustang. Something keeps nagging her in the back of her brain, but it will not pull to the front. Mac reaches for her bag and pulls out Sandra's sketch. There is something about this picture that bothers her, but she can't describe it. She is studying it when Spencer walks out of the bathroom, all dressed and ready to go. She glances at the sketch once more and packs it away as they make their way to the complimentary breakfast buffet.

While enjoying coffee and bagels, Spencer asks Mac what she sees when she studies Abby's sketch. "There is something about the picture that bothers me, but I can't describe it. The sketch looks familiar, but I don't know why. What about you? Does it remind you of anybody?"

"It does. Drake. But only a little. I want to ask Williams to check on Drake and find out where he's been during the murders. But Drake needs to remain unaware of our background check."

"Wow, Spencer. That will be a tricky conversation. I'll let you speak with Williams about Drake. Any word from Stubin or Baxter lately? And what about Fran's sketch?"

"No to both. I'll call later while we're riding as we can catch up with the rest of the members. I'll meet with Williams in person and speak with him about Drake. This might be another waste of time, but the sketch bothers me too." Spencer explains.

Mac fastens her seat belt as her phone rings. She glances at the readout and smiles when she sees it is her dad. How weird is that? He was on her mind this morning. "Hey, Dad. How are you? I was just thinking about you this morning."

Myles, relieved to hear Mac's voice, replies, "Good, Mac. How about you? Your safety is our primary concern and a major cause for worry. I found out yesterday about Zack Shelley. You heard about him, right?"

"I heard someone shot him, but we're still in Alabama. No one called us with an update last night. We're just now getting on the interstate to head back to Atlanta. Did he make it?"

"No. I'm afraid he passed. They shot him in his driveway, and he bled out just like the others. My understanding is the police got a good slug they can use for comparison. I'm sorry, Mac. I know this is hard on you. Please be careful. Your mom wants you to come for supper tonight. Bring Spencer. She just needs to see you."

"Okay, Dad. Let me check with him, and I'll call you back in a little while. We need to check in with Agent Williams. Thanks, Dad."

Mac ends the call and stares at her phone for several seconds, then she peeks at Spencer. With his eyes deep blue, she realizes he heard the conversation about Zack. "Can you believe another one? I wonder why the murdered agents were all shot and killed in their driveways. It must signify something, but what?"
Spencer doesn't have an answer to the question about the driveway, and he doesn't elaborate as he contemplates his conversation with Williams. Frustration has a hold on Spencer, and he doesn't want Mac to see him this frustrated, but this killer has him twisted in knots. It stumps him. He wants to be with Mac differently, more than just partners, but they must solve this case first. They ride in silence for over an hour.

With miles passing by, Spencer reaches for his cell phone. He calls Stubin first. They speak for about twenty minutes, each catching the other up on their respective sides of the investigation. Lacey talks about how she thought they had

had a good lead on a former agent the FBI released for insubordination.

Stubin says, "They couldn't locate the guy and thought he might be on the run. However, they tracked him down to his relatives in Florida. He was on vacation. Baxter and Lacey showed up at the guy's doorstep. Just about gave his wife a heart attack."

Spencer gets a delightful laugh at that one. "Is everything okay now?"

"Yes, it's worked out now, and he's no longer a lead." Then Spencer has his say. He tells Stubin about the green Mustang and the kid. Spencer feels like saying he just wasted two days tracking the kid down, but he doesn't. He keeps it to himself because he's trying to stay upbeat for Mac. Then Spencer asks about the Shelley murder and Fran's sketch.

Stubin answers, "We have a slug, and it should be in Atlanta by this afternoon. Williams wants Mac to inspect it before he turns it over to the lab. There's nothing new to report on Fran's sketch. Fran is having difficulty with it. She keeps making changes, so we're still waiting. I'm not sure how reliable it will be once we get our hands on it, anyway."

"Sounds good, Stubin. Tell the crew we're about an hour away. We'll come directly to the conference room."

"See you then."

Spencer shares Stubin's information with Mac.

Mac almost forgets to ask Spencer about supper with her father. "Can you have supper with my parents and me tonight?"

"I would love to have more of your mom's cooking." Spencer replies, then Mac sends her dad a quick text advising him they'll be glad to join them for supper.

On the last leg of their trip, Mac, and Spencer review the note cards. They want to make sure to list all the intel overlooking nothing. Mac adds information about the agents dying in their driveways.

Mac and Spencer pull into the parking lot at the FBI Atlanta office at 1100 sharp. The traffic was great. As they park, a patrol car passes them. They both stare at it. The driver appears vaguely familiar. Neither one speaks as the vehicle leaves the lot. Once it's gone, they search for the driver's name. There's no one in the parking lot to ask about it. They run into the lobby, and a group of agents, including Drake and Lacey, are stepping on the elevator. Spencer asks if anyone saw a patrol car in the parking lot about three minutes ago. All heads shake no. How were they going to find the driver? Maybe surveillance video will show them something.

Mac and Spencer take a ride up in the elevator to see Agent Williams. "Hi, Agent Williams. How are things? Any recent development on Zack's murder, and why wasn't he in a safe house?" Mac questions.

"Well, just who I was talking about. Zack was testifying in a trial when the murder happened. Please come with me. I want you to dissect a slug, and I want your opinion on something."

"Let's go." Williams leads Mac into his office. The slug lies on his desk in an evidence bag. He signs it, and then Mac signs her name to the chain of custody. She takes a pair of gloves from Agent Williams and places them on her hands. Then she picks up the magnifying glass.

"I can tell you the bullet is a 223 caliber. It appears to have similar or possibly the same striations as the other one. See this mark? This will match with the other slug. I'm confident we have a match. This is the same caliber of bullet that killed Mabry. If we can find the gun, we can get our killer."

"Great! Just what I wanted to hear. We must have something to tie the killer to the gun. Just like the rest of us, I want this killer captured now." Williams beams with the match.

Mac asks Williams, "Can I share something with you in private?"

Williams looks at her and says, "Of course you can. What's on your mind?"

Mac stammers and then proceeds. "The sketch from Abby and Sandra is familiar somehow. I think I've seen this guy, but I can't put a name to the face."

"You are the third person who has expressed the same thought to me. Everyone says they know this person, but no one can give me a name. I can tell you he looks familiar, but I don't have a name either." Williams shakes his head as he can't give a confident answer.

Mac shrugs her shoulders. "Oh well. It will come to me! Are the rest of the graduates in the safe house?"

"Yes, they are, but they're getting antsy. The graduates are tired of being trapped. They say now is the time to make a move so they can return home."

"I agree. I just wished I knew the next step. By the way, have we received Fran's sketch yet?"
Shaking his head side to side, he says, "No, we haven't. I emailed the sketch artist late yesterday but haven't received a reply yet. Fran is still making changes, so I'm unsure of its reliability once we receive it."
Williams leads Mac out of his office, and they walk back to the conference room together. Drake stands outside the room with Spencer when Mac and Williams walk to join the two. Mac tilts her head and studies Drake in a new light. She tries to compare him to the sketch. Yes, there are similarities, but he isn't the person in the picture. She hears Spencer telling Drake all about their trip.

Drake asks if Mac is going to the safe house, and Spencer states, "No, she is staying with me for the time being."

Spencer notices Mac and Williams walking his way, and he ends his conversation with Drake. Drake slowly walks past Mac and slightly rubs her arm on his way past. Mac ignores Drake's touch, but she wonders if Drake did it so she would talk to him. She enters the conference room without looking back. Drake stops at the next door, turns around, and watches as Mac steps into the room.

Chapter 9

The task force meets for the first time in five days. With so much to discuss, Williams caters lunch from The Varsity, an Atlanta landmark. The members enjoy hot dogs, onion rings, and the shop's famous orange drink. Then, when the food containers sit empty, they get down to business.

Stubin receives a text message, but he ignored it since the meeting started. Seconds later, he gets another one, and Williams asks him to answer it or silence his phone. Stubin steps outside for five minutes. Then he runs back into the room because he can't contain his news.

Williams sees the excitement on his face. "Well, are you going to share your news, or are you going to keep it yourself?"

Stubin says, "We have a solid lead. A few instructors recognized the sketched portrait, and they are searching for the file to ID the face. We might get a name by nightfall. I told Instructor Tipton I would call him later today if he hasn't called before then."

The team claps and settles into their seats for the rest of the meeting. Spencer and Mac share the events of the past two days. Abby's sketch was the biggest news. But there was also Fran's description of the man on the car's hood, and her description matched Abby's sketch. However, the task force still waits for Fran's sketch. Williams advises the group that a South Carolina agent, Colby Chastain, will join the task force tomorrow. He is working on two leads from Zack's neighbor.

After the meeting, Mac walks straight to her desk, feeling like she's been away for a long time instead of two days.

She wants to get busy with the updated ballistics since she now has something to compare. She jumps right in with the report on the slugs taken from the two agents and the one slug found in the tree at Mabry's murder. Mac works at the computer and creates her evidence book, for lack of a better word, into something usable. Mac has her way of comparing and analyzing ballistics. She begins at the bullet head and then continues down the casing. She catalogs and marks every groove and landing. Then she starts over and does it all again. The longitudinal striations must match. Once this satisfies her, she compares what she has with the FBI ballistics on file. She determines the round is a 223 caliber rifle round. Next, she searches the database for known matches based on the striations in the bullet casing. It matches with the Remington 223, including load capacity and grain. In her mind and gut, she surmises a law enforcement officer bears the responsibility for these murders. Now Mac and the team must figure out the shooter's identity.

Since the Remington is the weapon of choice for most law enforcement officers because ammunition is plentiful and less expensive than other brands, this isn't a surprise. The grain and load capacity for the latest slug is a match to the FBI's data. Mac makes a note to check on that tidbit of information. As she finishes, she hears Spencer calling her name.

Mac jumps up and races to Spencer. He sees her coming. "What is it? Why are you in such a hurry?"

"Come on. Williams called. We have to get back to the conference room! Williams said we have something, and we'll like it!"

Mac and Spencer run to the elevator. Mac's heart pounds in her chest. She wants to get to the conference room in a hurry. With the elevator stopped on the floor below, they bolt for the stairs since Williams waits for them. They take seats closest to the door, albeit a little out of breath. The members around the table stare at them, but no one bothers to ask why they are out of breath. Mac and Spencer glance at one another and shrug their shoulders, wondering why everyone stares at them when they got here as fast as they could.

Williams calls the meeting to order. "We have a break. Our search centers on John Honeycutt. They dismissed him from the FBI academy for his lack of ability because his shooting and math skills were a little off. Honeycutt was arrogant, and he didn't take constructive criticism well. However, the FBI offered him a desk job at headquarters. But he turned it down, and his parting words to Special Agent Burke were not professional. Burke kept his written notes from his meeting with Honeycutt, and an agent investigating Burke's murder found it in a file in a locked drawer in his desk. The agents have tried to find Honeycutt to question his whereabouts during the murder, but he's missing. The interesting part is he lives in Atlanta."

Stubin raised his hand. "What class did he attend? I don't remember his name. And how long has he been away?" Stubin thumbed through a few rosters.

"He attended four classes back. We dispatched a patrol unit to Honeycutt's house, and they found unopened mail in his mailbox. It appears he's been away for over a month, and that left his house unoccupied. The agents working on Burke's case are coming to Atlanta. They're getting a search warrant for Honeycutt's house."

Spencer asks, "What time will they execute the warrant? I'd love the opportunity to be a part of that one."

Williams grins. "1500. All are welcome. Next, we are getting a photo of Honeycutt to all of you, and we're emailing one to Fran and Abby. We'd like both ladies to see if they recognize Honeycutt. Spencer and Mac will handle that for us since you've already contacted both Fran and Abby."

"Glad to do it, sir." Spencer nods his head as Williams dismisses the group.

On their return to their office, Mac questions Honeycutt's motive. "Why did Honeycutt wait all this time to kill Burke and the other agents? Why this class of graduates?" Her head moves from side to side as she tries to fathom an idea.

"Maybe it took him this long to put it all together and figure out a plan. Although, you would think he'd have a tie to this last class. Why make it so personal?"

"My point exactly. This is personal. Why pick us? I'll call dad and see if I^2 can come up with anything."

Mac grabs her phone from her desk and notices several calls from a restricted number. The caller left no messages, just missed calls. She skims over the notifications and taps the speed dial button for her dad, the king of the private investigation world. Spencer listens as he talks with her dad. Mac tries her best to convince her dad of her safety. He wants her to stay at his house or go to a safe house. All she wanted was information, and here he is doing his fatherly thing. Spencer can't imagine being in Myles's place, knowing his only daughter is a target for a killer, and he is helpless to stop it. Mac turns toward Spencer, and her face shows her emotions. Her mouth is downturned, and her eyes hold unshed tears. She's a ball of nerves. Her family causes emotional turmoil for her sometimes by twisting her emotions. She always wants to please her dad, but this time she can't. She'll not go in hiding. Her determination will win this battle.

"Give it to me. What did your dad say? Other than he wants you in the safe house, and I agree." Spencer lifts his hand to show Mac he isn't finished speaking yet. "But we both know that isn't happening. So is he going to search for this John Honeycutt?"

"Yes, he'll help. He took down the request while I was on the phone with him." Then, Mac's phone rings. She glances down, and the phone says, "Restricted call." As she looks at Spencer with her eyebrows lifted, she questions her next move.

Without considering the ramifications, Spencer says, "Answer it."

Mac answers the call, then she listens to heavy breathing. She says hello repeatedly until the connection dies.

With his eyebrows together and a concerned tone, Spencer inquires, "Mac, you're pale. What's going on?"

"I've been receiving calls that come across my phone as a *restricted caller*, and I haven't answered them. Today, they started coming more often. I was afraid it would be something like this. Please tell me it has nothing to do with our case."

Spencer's eyes turn dark. Without an answer, he says, "let's go to the lab and ask them to trace the call. Have you spoken to Agent Williams about this?"

"No," Mac explains. "No one knows. I kept it to myself because I hoped it would stop." Mac's insides turn to mush. This emotional turmoil is just too much to handle. She regrets not telling Spencer or her dad about these calls. Her dad would have known what to do.

"Let's drop in on Agent Williams. He needs updating as soon as possible."

With a death grip on her phone, Mac asks, "Will you go upstairs with me? I'm a little shaken." She rubs the back of the phone while staring at it.
"Yes. We'll go by Williams's office first, then make our way down to the lab. I want to see if they can tell us anything about the call."

Mac and Spencer visit Williams's office. He's on the phone with Reagan, updating her on the newest revelations. When he notices the expressions on their faces, it causes concern because its obvious something happened. He waves them into his office. Once they sit, he quickly finishes up his call.

"Reagan is working on new intel and updating the profile. She feels Honeycutt is Burke's killer, but she isn't sure about the graduates. She said he fits the profile, but it concerns her that this info came so easily. And Honeycutt has no connection to the recent graduates. We'll deal with that later. Now, what's on your mind?"

Spencer waves his arm at Mac and directs his head toward Williams. He prompts her to speak. These phone calls could be a precursor to something more sinister. How can he get Mac to trust him? Why hadn't she mentioned the calls?

Mac clears her throat and says, "I've received phone calls for the last week or so. The caller ID says *restricted caller*, and I've ignored them until today. I answered at Spencer's suggestion, and all I heard was heavy breathing. No background sounds. No, nothing." Mac's eyes hold steady as she speaks with Williams, but her leg bounces in a rapid cadence.

Williams glares at her. "Why haven't you told someone? You've been hip-to-hip with Spencer for weeks now. I take it by the expression on Spencer's face he was unaware too. Why?"

Mac gives in, and her eyes turn down as she tries to explain. "I never considered the killer would come after me, and why would he? I haven't been with the FBI long enough to garner enemies—or so I thought. Besides, Spencer has been so wrapped up in the case. I didn't want to trouble him. Especially if the calls just stopped coming." Mac sighed, waiting for Williams' rebuttal.

Williams continues, "Let me explain something. When we have things happen out of the ordinary, we share. No matter how trivial. These phone calls have the potential to be dangerous. Is it fair to leave your partner in the dark? Consider how you would feel if Spencer did the same to you."

"No, sir. I apologize. I should have brought it to Spencer and then shared it with you as soon as it started. It won't happen again." Mac stated.

Agent Williams stands and walks around his desk. "Mac, you're a special person. I would like to keep you around for a while. Please stay close to Spencer. Or better yet, go to a safe house or your parents' house. You're the only graduate not in lockdown."

"I'm not running anywhere. We're going to the lab to see if they can find anything on the last call. Spencer mentioned something about back tracing."

Williams nods his head, yes. "Well then, get going. The quicker, the better."
Mac and Spencer stroll to the lab. Spencer speaks with the tech staff and tells them what happened. They take Mac's phone and start working their magic. They say they'll call Spencer once the information is available.

The elevator dings, and Mac and Spencer step out and into the path of Drake. It shocks him to be in Mac's space. He tries to step back, but someone blocks his retreat.

Drake asks, "How are things going? Any word on the suspect yet? I heard about this, John Honeycutt." He glances around as he tries again to move to the side, but people surround him.

Spencer steps from behind Mac and states, "Just a few items added to the list. We haven't found Honeycutt yet. When are you going to the gym? I need a spotter."

"I was thinking about going sometime this week. It's been hard to find the time since we are running in all directions. We'll try to meet up soon. I need to work off stress too."

Spencer answers, "Let me know, and I'll meet you there."

With the excitement surrounding Mac's phone calls, Williams texts a reminder to Spencer about the search warrant for Honeycutt's house. Since he can't make it, he wants their eyes on it. So, they drive over to Honeycutt's house to see if anything turns up for their investigation. Spencer asks Chastain if he'd like to tag along.

"I'd love to. It will get me out of the office for a bit." Chastain replied.

Chastain slides into the back. Once the drive begins, the group shares some of their earlier years on the drive. Chastain shares the story of how he joined the FBI right out of college. He was in his last finance class when his professor asked him to stay back after class. Chastain admits to being a little nervous even though there was no reason.

A guy dressed in a dark suit with a white shirt entered the room after everyone had cleared out. Chastain describes the meeting that changed his life. The guy in the suit was big and burly but had a sugar piece underneath. He explained what the FBI looks for in an agent and his responsibilities with the agency. Chastain left that meeting in a stupor. With graduation coming, he had too much on his mind. He finished up his studies, becoming the valedictorian of his class. During his move from school back to his parent's place, he misplaced the agent's card. Two weeks after graduation, the agent knocked on his parents' front door, and the rest was history. "My goal was to major in finance and work in a bank like my uncle, but the FBI came calling, and I never looked back. I'm not married, but I have a girlfriend. We talk about getting married, but neither of us has made a move."

"Sounds like we can use you, Chastain. Financials are always a topic for us. How about digging into Honeycutt's financials? I'd like to know if someone paid him to kill the agents."

"I'll start on it once we return from his house. Thanks, Spencer." Chastain turns his head and surveys the area outside the window.

The group arrives at their destination amid a barrage of law enforcement vehicles. With entry complete, agents are perusing the inside and outside of the house. The trio enters the house with gloves and booties. Mac questions a crime scene tech. "Anything of interest?"

"Nothing yet. We're searching for a gun but haven't located one. By the looks of the house, he hasn't been home in a month or so." The tech shakes his head in disappointment.

Williams calls Spencer about the entry, and Spencer places his phone on speakerphone. Spencer confirms they're inside the house now, then he says, "Williams, Chastain agreed to dig into Honeycutt's financials for us since we want proof if someone paid him to murder our agents,"

"Good call. I hear Chastain is an expert with the paper."

"I'm not sure about an expert, sir, but I do like searching for the inappropriate behavior that people find themselves. If it's there, I'll find it," Chastain states into the phone with a confident stare.

Williams concludes the call by stating he will meet the group at the office for an update on Honeycutt's house inspection.

Once they inspected the house, the trio made their way to the office. They discuss viable reasons the killer might have for the murders. Chastain asks to look at the murder board. He hasn't taken the time to study it since he arrived. Mac advises she'll work on ballistics when they return, and she'll be happy to escort him to the conference room for a bit of study time. Chastain chuckles. "It sounds like I'm back in school."

The conference room is empty when they return, so Chastain has the table and the board to himself. He jots notes on paper and gets Honeycutt's personal information. Then he opens his laptop for a few hours of financial investigation. Frustration grips Chastain as he pours through site after site, searching through Honeycutt's finances, which isn't much.

Mac suggests to Spencer they go over the ballistics while Chastain works on the financials. She's ready to show Spencer her findings. They head into their office, and Mac shuts the door.
Spencer looks at her and says, "Why are you acting this way? You seem mad."

"No, I'm not acting, anyway. You know I'm not comfortable around Drake, and I don't want him to know I've returned from Honeycutt's house."

Spencer turns his stare toward her computer. Mac witnesses the anxiousness creep into his eyes. Boy, she loves those eyes. The more she's with them, the more she likes them. Mac shakes her head, trying to clear it. She needs to focus on the task at hand. They need to capture this suspect—the sooner, the better. Mac sits down at her computer and tries to open her program. She clicks the icon, and a warning flashes across the page. The computer screen boasts black background with big, bold white letters, and the only word on it is "Bang!"

Chapter 10

Mac is speechless. With her eyes zeroed in on the computer, she doesn't hear Spencer. She can't take her eyes away from the warning.

Spencer walks over to her because he wants to know what is so important that she can't respond. He pauses, understands the urgency of the situation, and then jumps into overdrive. He calls the crime lab downstairs.

"Hey, Charlie, I need you in my office now. Bring your fingerprint stuff. We have a crime scene!" Spencer barks. He ends the call without waiting for a reply.

Next, he notifies Agent Williams. Spencer touches Mac to bring her back. She's pale and her body trembles. Spencer doesn't want to leave her alone, so he says, "Follow me. We're going to the video room. I want to see who has been on this floor within the last few hours."

Mac can't rationalize a thought. After regaining her sense of composure, she says, "How could someone enter the FBI office and put this on my computer undetected?" First the phone calls, now the computer warning. Mac runs her fingers through her hair.

"I don't know. Someone might have placed it on the computer from inside the building or sent the page via the internet. We'll leave it to the cyber guys. Charlie is coming up here. Oh, here he is now. Hey, Charlie."

"Hey, Spencer. How is there a crime scene up here?" Charlie questions with a quizzical expression as he surveys the area.

Spencer waves his hand toward their office and says, "This way." He enters first and invites the other two inside, and then he takes the lead by explaining what Mac found on her computer.

"Well, scoot over, and let me have a look." Charlie touches the mouse with gloves on his hands, and the sign-in screen appears. There is no black screen with white letters. It vanished!
Charlie glances up at Spencer with the same puzzled expression. "Is this the right computer? There is nothing on here like what you described."

Spencer and Mac yell, "It was there!"

With his hands in the air, "I believe you, but it's not here, now." Charlie explains.

Mac continues, "Sorry, Charlie. I saw it first. Then Spencer came over and witnessed it. I only touched the computer to sign in." Mac sinks into her chair. Is she losing her mind? It was there! Spencer saw it too. This killer is trying to drive her crazy.

Williams says, "Charlie, take the computer to the lab, and tell me how this happened. I want your answer yesterday."

Charlie slipped out of the office with Mac's computer in hand. He didn't speak on his way out because he could feel the tension.

"Mac, I have to make this call. You're going into protective custody because we can't take the chance. You pick the place. Spencer, you go with her if you can. If she stays with her parents, it's their decision if you can stay overnight. If you chose a safe house, each house has a protection detail assigned, but it can't hurt to have another person around."

Mac sinks further in the chair. She can't offer a response because she is dumbfounded. How did this happen?

Spencer says, "Sir, I want to go to the video room. I want to check this floor for visitors. If they did it in person, their picture would be on the video. If they did it remotely, Charlie would come up with something."

Williams agrees as he barks instructions. "Get Mac out of here. Text me your destination."

Mac leans her head out the office door and asks, "Charlie, is it possible to send the ballistics presentation from my computer to Spencer's email?"

Charlie replies, "I'll send it as soon as I get to the lab."

Then Mac turns to Spencer, "So should we go to stay at my parents' house or go to a safe house?"

Spencer thinks about it and says, "It's time we call your dad. He needs updating on today's events. Let's get his suggestion. I imagine he'll ask you to go to his house."

Reluctantly, Mac agrees. They walk back into their office in silence. Spencer goes first, surveys the office, and finds nothing out of place. Mac follows and sits at her desk while she calls her dad to explain the situation. She tells him about the phone calls, the computer screen, and John Honeycutt. She shares with him all the information they know.

As she ends her update, her dad gets his turn to speak. "Mac, you and Spencer grab your things, and you can stay at the house. I'm coming your way, and I should be there in fifteen minutes. We'll follow you home. We're not taking any chances as this guy is way too close. Call me when you leave the office and head to the parking lot. And honey, I'm glad you called me. See you soon."

Mac's call ended with her eyes down because they glisten with unshed tears. Mac can't take the chance of peering into Spencer's eyes because she knows her tears will fall. She keeps telling herself no tears, but she's unsure how much longer she can hang on. She has experienced nothing like this before. Nor does she want to, ever again.

Spencer walks over to her and places his hand on her shoulder. Just the touch does it to him now. The heat rises from the core of his body. He wants to hold her tight and never let go. He wants to be her protector. Once again, he keeps his thoughts to himself, but it's harder and harder. One day, he'll talk about his feelings, and he won't be able to stop until they're all on the table. However, he knows it can't be now because they must live through this ordeal first.

Mac touches Spencer's hand as it rests on her shoulder. He takes her hand, and they hold hands for a few seconds. Probably a few seconds too long. He's her rock. She accepts it now. Since she's learning how to deal with actual pressure, she desperately needs someone by her side.

"I guess we're going to my parents." Dad will escort us, and he'll meet us in the parking lot. Then, they'll follow us to the house. We need to stop and get our clothes and whatever else we need."

Spencer grabs his laptop. He says, "I have what I need from here. We'll stop at my apartment for our things."

Mac stands to leave and says, "Oh no. Spencer, the note cards. Where are they?"

"Don't panic. They are still in my bag."

"Can you check? Just to make sure. It takes a lot of effort to complete the cards." Mac pleads.

Spencer says, "Hold on." He steps over to his side of the office and pulls his bag off the floor. He reaches into the side pocket and removes two stacks of cards. "Here they are, Mac. Just like we left them. Now let's get going."

Williams catches up with them on their way out. "Still nothing on Honeycutt. Somehow, he vanished. The agents investigating Agent Burke's death confirmed Honeycutt has a 223 caliber rifle registered to him. Burke wrote several negative comments in Honeycutt's file about his lack of ability to shoot long range. Honeycutt had a hard time learning how to decipher scope settings. Agents also found Honeycutt hung out with a guy by the name of Seth Campbell. Seth is in the wind too. The agents want to speak with him and see if he has information about Honeycutt's whereabouts. They have located no living family members. Well, the day is dwindling, and I want you situated by dark. Did you decide where you're staying?"

Mac answers, "Yes, we're staying with my parents. I've already spoken to dad, and the entourage is waiting. We're running by Spencer's for our clothes and then traveling north."

"OK. Check in with me. I'll update you as soon as we receive additional information." Williams turns and heads for his office to meet with Chastain.

Mac and Spencer hit the parking lot at a dead run. Spencer surveys the area to make sure no one aims at Mac. Mac is in tactical mode. Her eyes scan the lot from side to side.

Spencer asks Mac, "Hey, is that your dad's black Suburban? Let me go up to our car first. We need to look under it for a bomb or tracking device on it."

Speaking over her shoulder, Mac replied, "Yes, dad is in the car. He said he would make it, and he did. Let me speak with him first."

Mac walks over to the Suburban, and the window slides downward. "Hey, Mac. We swept your car, and it's clean. We didn't find any trace of a bomb or tracking device. My guy here will start it remotely. Let him have the keys."

Spencer hands them over, keeping Mac between the vehicle and his body. This move shielded her from the parking lot and the tops of the building. The car starts, and nothing unexpected happens. Mac and Spencer steal a glance at each other, and Mac lets out a sigh.

Spencer says, "Let's get going. I need to get you behind closed doors to safety."

An hour later, they pull into the driveway leading to Mac's parents' house. They spend their time playing with the dogs and enjoying supper with the family. Even Mac's brothers show up for the event. Spencer plays pool with her brothers as they make small talk while Mac spends time with her parents. Mac's mom worries about her daughter, and the worry lines etched in her mom's forehead prove it. Mac tells her mom she's going upstairs to her dad's office to see if he's uncovered anything, then she strolls up the stairs to the loft area.

The word *loft* is not the best word to describe this room because it encompasses many square feet. Myles spends a ton of time up here. It has all the comforts of an office. Computer's line one wall, and a smattering of machines sit in the middle of the room on a massive island. His favorites are the fingerprint, shoe print, and blood analysis systems. These are compact versions of the same systems in the lab at his corporate office, and they designed the systems just for him. They're the most high-tech analysis machines in the country. Police departments from all over the country send their evidence to I^2 for analysis. This firm is far more advanced in technology and schooled investigators than most. Mac loves to watch and listen as these machines work their magic. She enters the office and sees that her dad is on the phone. He waves her in, and she takes a seat in one of the high-back leather chairs and waits for him to finish. She glances around the room and notices her case is up on a computer on the wall. Her dad made a murder book too.

Mac points to it, and her dad nods his head, yes. The mouse slides across the desktop to bring the computer to life. The slideshow is worth watching twice, and she writes notes about additional information her dad needs to add. Honeycutt is another topic for her dad. Hopefully, there is something to that. Not sure why Honeycutt would come after her. It makes little sense. She reminds herself to read Honeycutt's bio. There must be a reason for him to set his sights on her and her classmates.

While waiting for her dad to end his call, her temporary cell phone rings. Her real one sits in the lab at the FBI office in

Atlanta while Charlie tries to find the number that keeps calling her. She glances down at the caller ID screen and holds her breath.

She answers on the third ring. "Hi, Mac. They triangulated the cell phone call to your phone to Centennial Olympic Park. So whoever is calling you is here in Atlanta and watching you," Agent Williams shares.

"Oh, wow. Did Charlie have anything to say about the computer issue?"

"He confirmed a few minutes ago that someone sent the message electronically. At least the person wasn't in the office. Charlie is working on the IP address for the sending computer, but he says it bounced across several continents, so he's not holding out much hope of finding the sender. Just stay close to your parents' house. Is Spencer still there?"

"Yes, he's downstairs with my brothers. Shall I get him for you?"

"No, just make sure you explain the cell phone call and the computer issue. Then, I'll have the lab tech put your phone back on your desk."

"Thanks, I will get it tomorrow." Mac agrees.

"Oh no, you won't! You're not coming back until we get this guy. Spencer can pick it up for you," Williams instructs.

"I understand. Talk to you soon." They disconnect their call. Mac leans back in the chair, trying to make sense of all of this. So, the caller is in Atlanta, and someone transmitted the warning electronically.

Myles, Mac's dad, looks over at her and asks, "What was all that about?"

At the same time, Spencer shows up at the door. He asks, "What was what about?"
Mac chuckles because she couldn't control it. She explains what Williams relayed to her about the phone call and the computer warning when she settles down.

They say at the same time, "I don't like it."

Mac giggles again. "Oh, wow. I hope you two don't keep doing that. You two are so funny!"

Spencer laughs and says, "Hey, have you heard the saying great minds think alike!"

Myles grins, but his mind is on the situation. "Let's talk. Is there any recent information I don't have in my murder book?"

Mac takes it upon herself to answer. "Yes, we found out a little more about John Honeycutt today. The problem is no one can find him. He has no family listed either. He hung around one friend, and he's missing too. I can't remember his name without looking at my cards."

Spencer butts in. "Seth Campbell—that's the friend's name."

"Yeah. Seth Campbell. I'm unsure if Williams found anything on him. He didn't mention it if he has."

Spencer answers a call from Chastain. He listens and shakes his head. When the call ends, he shares the news. Chastain found no large deposits made into Honeycutt's accounts. Honeycutt's finances are bleak. However, he receives a social security check from his father. At least that's what Chastain thinks. It's not much, but apparently, it's enough money for Honeycutt. If he killed Burke, he did it out of enjoyment, not for money.

Myles sits there without speaking, but his brain is in overdrive. A few seconds later, he says he'll join the search for Honeycutt and Campbell.

"Spencer, when you go back to the office, can you get a date of birth on this Campbell? There is more than one Seth Campbell in the US. I want to make sure I 'm searching for the right one."

Spencer replies, "I can make that happen without a trip to the office. Let me make a call."
Spencer turns and steps from the room. Six minutes later, he reenters and gives Myles the unwelcome news. No date of birth is available.

Myles studies Spencer. "You sure work fast."

"Thanks," says Spencer with a grin on his face. "I just wish it was better news."

Myles turns around and starts typing. He enters what information he has into his computer and states, "Now we wait."

Since he was in wait mode, Myles steps outside to play with his pups, and then it's off to bed. He bids good night to Mac and Spencer and leaves them alone in the office.

Mac and Spencer sit in silence for a while. Then Spencer speaks, "I'm leaving now. I'll return tomorrow afternoon. If you need anything, call."

Mac asks, "Can you stay here tonight? It would be safer if you did, and besides, dad said you could."

"It's a little odd staying the night at your parents. I don't want your parents to think badly of me, even though I'm here because of work." Spencer fidgeted in his seat, trying to decide if he could stay.

"Come on, Spencer. They know what is going on or what we want to be going on. Anyway, we have mitigating circumstances. One more person in the house will be helpful." Mac pleads her case, and she is a skilled negotiator.

Spencer gives Mac the devilish grin she loves so much and says, "Okay. Just tell them you twisted my arm! I'll leave early in the morning. I want to be at the office at 0800 for the task force meeting."

"Deal," replies Mac, and she trots off to find her mom.

The following day, Mac sleeps until 0800. She walks downstairs to find Spencer left two hours ago for work. She's disappointed she didn't get to speak with him before he left. Mac's mom, Mary, finds her in the kitchen with disappointment on her face.

Mary asks her only daughter, "Honey, is there anything you need to share about your relationship with Spencer? You sure seem disappointed he isn't here this morning."

"I guess I'm a little disappointed he isn't here, but I'm not ready to step out and say anything about our relationship other than we're partners. I feel we're closer because of all the murders. It's kind of hard not to be, I guess, since we've spent a lot of time together."

Mary says, "I can tell you both like each other. When all this mess is over, you two can give your relationship a genuine chance." She pats Mac on the shoulder.

Mac eyes her mom. "You can tell that from being with us just a few hours?"

"Why yes, honey. A few things in life are obvious, like when two people share an attraction. You have a noble guy in Spencer. He adores you, and he spoke to your father last night after you went to bed."

"What did he and Dad talk about?" Mac cringed while waiting for the reply.

Mary grins and says, "You. It scares him to death that he'll lose you. He made dad promise to keep you safe." Mary giggled as she said it, remembering the look on Myles' face.

"Oh my. I hope dad wasn't mad at Spencer."

Mary shook her head. "No. No way was he mad at Spencer. He likes him and says he would be good for you." Mary smiles as she shared.

"Well, isn't that interesting? I'm proud of dad. Where is he anyway?"

Mary tells Mac her dad drove to his office, but he left guys in the front and back of the house. They were not to go outside for anything. Mac just stares at her mom.

"Are you kidding me? I can't play with the dogs outside. I'll go stir crazy sitting in here all day." Mac looks around the room as if she is in jail.

Mary tries to calm her because Mac will go bonkers. Mac has never been a sitter nor patient. Growing up, Mac was always busy. If Mac wasn't playing with her brothers, she was reading—and not just fun books. She would read books of all kinds. Her mind seemed to be continually working.

Mary says, "Your dad has a few things you can do for I^2. At least you'll have something to keep you occupied."

"Good. I'll shower and be ready for dad." After she dresses, she walks to her dad's office, ready to work for him.

Spencer calls Mac, and she answers on the first ring. "What are you doing?" Spencer inquires.

"Not much. I'm doing a little routine work for dad. At least it will keep me occupied. But I'd rather work the case with you. Anything new?" Mac lays her pen down and rubs her temple.

"Yes. Are you sitting?"

Mac tenses and answers, "Just tell me. What now?"

Spencer continues, "Get your dad on speakerphone."

Mac says, hold on, and she returns to the line in thirty seconds with Myles. Mac asks Spencer to continue.

Spencer says, "Someone shot an agent in South Georgia in the head last night while he was outside for a smoke. The scary part was he was in the driveway of a safe house when the shooting occurred."

Myles rages. "How does the suspect find the location of the safe houses? Does the FBI not change the locations of these houses often enough?" Myles can hardly speak with his jaws clenched so tight.

Spencer speaks in a low tone. He tries to remain calm for Mac, but Myles explodes. Spencer wants to hug Mac and tell her everything will be okay. But he can't tell her this over the speakerphone. "The agent graduated with you, Mac. His name is Jordan Sutter."

"Oh, Spencer. He was the agent I told you was getting married in September. I can't hold it together anymore because all I do is walk around, trying to put the pieces together. It's a given I can't stay locked up forever, and I can't be out working the case. I've never felt so helpless." Mac expressed her frustration over her situation.

"I know, Mac. We're working on it," Spencer answers with a tinge of concern in his voice.

After a moment of silence, "Spencer, I have a favor," Myles states.

"Sure, sir. What is it?" Spencer tenses as he waits for the favor. He doesn't want Myles asking him to leave Mac alone because that is something he will not do regardless of who asks.

"Send me your murder book. Whatever you have, including what Williams has on this Honeycutt guy. I don't believe he's the only killer. He may have killed Agent Burke, but I'm unsure about the others. It doesn't fit. There's no personal connection I can find anywhere. We have to go deeper. You can send what you have to my email and thanks." Myles explains his reasons.

"I'll send it right away. Mac suggested the same about the personal connection." Spencer gulps air because Myles's request is doable, and he can handle it pronto.

Mac tells Spencer she'll talk to him later. She leaves her dad in the loft and goes to her room. With her head resting on her pillow, tears flow. She isn't supposed to cry, but she can't hold the tears inside any longer. With Mac scared out of her mind, she wants Spencer to be here with her. These people she knew and thought would be around for a long time are now dead. They all talked about retiring from the FBI. Mac cries for Jordan's fiancée and the life they would never share. How can this person be so cruel? Is anybody that coldhearted? She eventually cries herself out and falls asleep. She sleeps hard, but she's restless as she dreams of herself running. Mac is unsure where she is or where she's running to or from. She wakes herself up enough to make her way back to the kitchen where she runs into her mom as she prepares lunch. Mac can't consider eating lunch with her stomach in knots.

Mary asks, "Are you okay? You're not alone in this. This situation has us worried and scared too."

"I'm scared, mom, and I've never been so scared in my life. I feel like I'm being watched all the time. When I reflect on the last few weeks, I realize the same sensation has been with me for a while, but I didn't pay any attention to it."

Mary places her hands over her mouth. "Have you told your dad yet?"

"I've told no one except you. It doesn't matter. There's no way to identify them, anyway. Maybe I'm overreacting, and it might be paranoia too." Even after Mac says it, she doesn't believe it because she senses someone watches her. She wishes she knew who it was and why.

"Talk to dad. If you don't, I will." Mary instructs as Mac shrugs her shoulders, then concedes she'll tell him. She walks off toward the office with her head hung low and her shoulders slumped. Mac has always felt on top of her game, but this melee has her defeated. People surround her to protect her, but how long can she stay locked away?

Chapter 11

Mac calls Spencer and asks about the caliber of the bullet that killed Jordan, and Spencer replies, "The bullet is a 223 caliber. Just like the rest. Jordan was walking the driveway while he smoked when a bullet struck him in the head. He bled out in the driveway before the ambulance arrived. The medical examiner is removing the slug as we speak. They had a hard time finding Jordan's parents because they were out of town. We should have their information within the next two hours. Also, there are agents in Macon right now scouring the scene. The remaining agents at the safe house are being moved tonight to another location. Drake and Cameron will handle the move."

"I can't believe this is still happening. How can someone do this to us? We should solve crimes against our country, not crimes against our agents. This makes little sense. I'm unsure Honeycutt is our guy because he relates to no one. I've never met him, nor does anyone else seem to know him. If someone targets a certain class of graduates, wouldn't there be an association of some sort?"

"I agree, Mac. Williams is meeting with the task force and the profiler tomorrow morning. He wants updates. Stubin and Baxter agree with you and your dad that Honeycutt is not the killer. They would like to speak with his friend, Seth Campbell. No one can find him either. I was hoping your dad would help."

Mac pauses and says, "dad looked into it late last night. He's at the office right now. He won't even let me play with the dogs outside, and I'm going stir crazy. Dad has me doing mundane chores for one of his cases."

Spencer replied, "Well, at least it's something. Go back over your note cards and see what pops. I'll keep you up to date on what is happening here. Oh, I forgot to tell you Drake asked about you, and he wanted to see how you are coping."

Mac sucks in a deep breath and says, "Great. Now he's trying to be friends. He still bothers me. Call me if you hear anything."

"Okay. We'll talk later."

Mac reviews her notes and completes work for her dad. She jots several questions down for her case. She wants to review the class this Honeycutt attended. The entire class needs ruling out. Is Honeycutt related to someone at the FBI? While Mac works that angle, her cell phone rings. She just knows it's Spencer with an update. She grabs it without checking the caller ID and says, "Hello."

Then her blood turns ice cold as she listens to heavy breathing. No one speaks. She listens for two minutes, trying to pick up on any sounds. When she hears nothing discernable, she ends the call and dials Spencer. She tells him what happened. He tries to console her the best he can from a distance. This entire episode is consuming his whole being because it's hard to control the unexpected. There's nothing he wouldn't do to find this guy and put a bullet in his head for what he is doing to Mac.

"OK. Calm down. Let me call Williams and find out who has your new number. The phone is in the FBI bank of numbers. I'm uncertain who has access to the list. I'll call you back once I speak with Williams."

Mac disconnects and calls her dad. "I got another phone call. Same as before. Heavy breathing. No talking. No sounds. I stayed on the phone for two minutes, hoping to pick up on sounds, but I heard nothing." Mac sighs as she settles herself with a deep breath.

"I can't believe this. I'll bring you one of my phones. There is no way the FBI has this number. Sit tight a little while. We're still trying to get a lead on Seth Campbell. My phone is ringing. Let me take it, and I'll call you back. Don't go outside." Myles states.

"OK. Thanks, dad." Mac ends the call and stares at her phone. How can a simple telephone cause someone's pulse to race?

Stubin races into the FBI Atlanta office with news. His information might break this case wide open and move them to closure. Stubin rounds the corner and almost plows over Baxter. "Hey, Baxter, come on. We have to find Agent Williams. I have news."

"He's in the conference room on the eighth floor, staring at the murder board."

"Let's go. Time is wasting." Stubin enters the conference room in a sprint, followed by Bater.

"Williams, the Volusia County Sheriff's Office called me, and they have our Honeycutt guy. He was on vacation in Daytona Beach, and the police arrested him for public disorderly down by the boardwalk. Honeycutt was drunker than a skunk, and he was running his mouth. He let it slip about the murder of FBI agents—told the bartender how cool it was to shoot a powerful FBI agent. The bartender called the sheriff's office, and Deputy Rands called me because of our BOLO on Honeycutt."

Williams grins ear to ear. "It's about time we catch a break. Now we just have to get him to talk to us when he's sober, which should be interesting."

"How should we handle it? Should we go to Florida to interview him or extradite him to Atlanta?"

Williams pauses for a few seconds. "We need answers now. Not later. You and Baxter leave immediately and interview Honeycutt. If he's been in Florida all this time, then he's not our shooter, but verify Honeycutt's lodging arrangements while you are down there. We also need info on this, Seth Campbell. Has anyone found him yet?"

Stubin and Baxter share a glance, then both turn to Williams and shake their heads no.
"Go to Florida. Get me answers!"
Stubin and Baxter exit the conference room and head straight for their desks. Once the arrangements with the Volusia County Sheriff's Office are complete, they leave the building. On their way out, they run into Drake as he's returning from Macon. They involved him in the agent's transportation from one safe house to another.

Drake asks Stubin, "What's the rush?"

Stubin answers, "Honeycutt is in the Volusia County Sheriff's Office jail. He's been on vacation in Daytona Beach, Florida, where he must have traveled after Burke's shooting. We're on our way to interview him now. We'll report back later."

"Be safe," mutters Drake as he stares after them.

Stubin let Baxter drive. He uses the downtime to call Spencer and Mac and bring them up to date. As Baxter pulls out of the lot, they watch Drake run to his car.

"Where is he going in such a hurry?" Stubin points to Drake.

"Who knows?" replies Baxter. "Let's concentrate on getting this car down the road. We have at least seven hours of drive time without traffic. We need a plan to get this guy to talk to us. By the time we arrive, he'll be completely sober. It concerns Williams that Honeycutt will stop talking once he sobers. I hope he doesn't get a lawyer before we can get to him."

Stubin chuckles. "I sure wish we could have talked to him while he was drunk. We would have our answer now." A picture forms in Stubin's mind of him interrogating Honeycutt and winning. Stubin smiles.

After a few minutes of silence, Stubin plucks his cell phone from his pocket and pushes the button for Spencer. Spencer answers on the second ring. "Hey, Spencer, Stubin here. We have news. We're on our way to Daytona Beach to speak to Honeycutt."

"Daytona? It must be nice to get a beach trip. Why Daytona?"

Stubin explains, "Honeycutt has been in Daytona for weeks now, and a sheriff's deputy arrested him this afternoon for public disorderly. Drunk off of his butt was the way the deputy described him. Honeycutt mentioned something about the FBI murders while he was at a boardwalk bar. A bartender called the sheriff's office and said he didn't know if this guy was just spouting off, but the police arrested him based on our BOLO. They are holding him for us."

"That sounds great. This might be the break we're waiting for. With Honeycutt being in Daytona for weeks, I guess that proves he's not our shooter. Interesting. When you locate Honeycutt's hotel, that will solidify his alibi. So, now, we should concentrate on finding Seth Campbell."

"Honeycutt's relationship with Seth is our first question. We want Seth's location or how we can contact him. We'll let you know as soon as we have spoken to him. We're going straight to the sheriff's office."

"Thanks for the update, guys. I'll tell Mac." Spencer and Stubin end their call, and Spencer doesn't even put his phone down before he dials Mac. She answers as soon as she reads his number.

"Tell me something good, please!" Mac says when she answers.

"I have news for you. I just hope it leads to the breakthrough we have been needing." Spencer tells her about the developments with Honeycutt.

"It sounds good to have a solid lead. Stubin is one guy that can get him to talk. My fear is Honeycutt will lawyer up once he hears the FBI is coming to town." Mac doodles on her paper while she considers Honeycutt. Why isn't anything ever easy?

"Be patient a little while longer. Once I finish here, I'll head your way. Stubin said he would call as soon as he and Baxter finish with Honeycutt. He also suggested you email him questions for Honeycutt. He'll review them while they are driving."

"OK. Can't wait to see you. Be careful." Mac ponders the questions she would like to ask Honeycutt. First, where is Seth, and how does he relate to this class? Are Honeycutt and Seth related or just friends? Mac calls her dad and shares the latest information on Honeycutt.

Myles soaks up the information. He tells Mac he'll be home soon, and they'll talk. With his case knowledge, he assumes Seth Campbell is the shooter, but the connection remains a mystery.

Myles pulls up his computer search of all Seth Campbell's in the southeast United States. The entries have corresponding age descriptions. There are thirty-eight men in five states that match. He'll try to find all thirty-eight himself if he has to. He calls Spencer and says, "Spencer, this is Myles."

"Hi, sir. What's wrong?" Myles grins, knowing Spencer is worried about Mac. Myles continues,

"I found thirty-eight Seth Campbell's in five southeastern states. If you're not busy, I could use your help to make phone calls tonight, if you're available."

"As a matter of fact, I'm on my way to your house now. I would love to help. Have you updated Mac?"

Myles replies, "No, not yet. I just pulled the search information from my computer."

"I won't say anything until you tell her. She'll want to help too."

"Good. I was hoping she would be in a better mood tonight," Myles said, remembering her response after

120

learning of Jordan's death. "See you soon." Myles ends the call.

Spencer takes a call from Williams because they executed the search warrant for Honeycutt's place. Since Williams couldn't make it to the scene, they needed to discuss it. The duo reviews the evidence. The house had been dark and dirty. No one had stayed in that place for at least a month, if not longer. Spider webs and dust mites began playing in the noncirculating air as they ransacked the home. They found no rifle in the search. Where was his gun?

Spencer pulls into the driveway amid the black Suburban's parked in the street. He glances around the property for the entourage because he didn't see the guys in the back. He exits his car, and the front door to the house flies open. Mac stands on the threshold in plain view of the world.

Spencer barks, "Close the door and put yourself on the inside. Now." Mac follows Spencer's instructions but with fear on her face. Spencer hates to scare her, but the security detail for the backyard is missing. Anytime a vehicle arrives, all security personnel checks on the newcomers just to make sure they belong. He walked the perimeter of the house and found no one on patrol. Now concern creeps into his face. Once he returns to the vehicles parked out front, he asks for their counterparts' status. Two guys sit inside the SUV. Spencer knocks on the window, and the window slides down halfway. Spencer questions the guys about their rear security detail. Then he advises he walked the perimeter and saw no one in the back of the house. The security guys look at each other and exit the vehicle at a dead run. Spencer stops at the front door and asks Mac to call her dad because they might need backup. Then, Spencer trots through the house and exits the back door.

"Over here." George, the security team lead, points to the ground. "This lighter belongs to David. He would never leave it. His wife gave it to him several years ago," he says. "This isn't good. I assigned David to the backyard about three hours ago. He checked in one hour ago with an all-clear per the logbook. We need to keep searching."

"Over here, guys." This request comes from George's partner, Josh. "Those appear to be drag marks." Josh points at a set of tracks. "But they stop right here. I don't see any tire marks or anything after they stop." Josh turns with his head down, inspecting the ground for more evidence.

Spencer adds, "Are there shoe prints? Someone might have thrown him over their shoulders and walked him out."

George motions. "You're right, Spencer. Here they are." George points to the shoe prints on the ground. He also finds broken twigs in the same area.

"Don't touch them. Mark them with something, and we'll let Myles handle the collection. He has the lab that can process the prints without the wait."

Spencer's mind is reeling. This guy must be brave because he enters Myles's property, or he isn't familiar with Myles yet. Sure wouldn't want to be this guy when Myles gets a hold of him. Spencer asks the guys, "Who knows Mac is staying here?"

George hears him and says, "Are you talking to us? Or are you talking to yourself? Because I have no idea what the FBI has on this case. Myles asked us to keep a watch over Mac because of the FBI murders. We have read no files or anything. But someone knows the ins and outs of your operation. I can state that as a fact."

"Yeah. Those are my thoughts too. But I have no idea who. We have a small task force, and they know the agents' locations, but none of them were in the class with Honeycutt or Seth. No one claims to know Honeycutt or Seth. The task force members have been around the agency for years, except for Mac. Anyway, most of the task force members are from out of town."

Spencer's cell phone rings. He recognizes Mac's new number, and he answers it on the first ring. "Hey, we're in the woods behind your house. I'm walking toward the house now. No, everything is fine. Be there in a few."

George listens to the conversation and tilts his head to the side and lifts an eyebrow. "Are you going to tell her what happened to David?"

"I'll defer to her dad to share the news because I don't want to step on anyone's toes, especially Myles. He should be here soon. We can't afford to lose the daylight we have left."

"Go ahead to the house. I'll keep snooping. Josh will go back to the front of the house while I'm back here." Josh heard the George's directive and began his trek to the front.

Spencer glances around, "Keep alert. He might still be here."

George replies, "That is a strong possibility. Would he camp out in the woods? If so, we can conduct a grid search." George walks further into the woods surveying the area. Then turns toward Spencer since he didn't receive a reply.

Spencer is unsure how to answer George's question, so he shrugs his shoulders and makes his way to the house while going over the case in his head. It has to be someone close to the investigation, but who? That is the question of the century. Mac waits at the door when he arrives.

Instantly she probes him with questions. "What's going on? Why is everyone in the backyard by the woods? I saw you back there with George."

"Where is your dad? He said he would be here by now."

"Are you trying to change the subject?" inquires Mac.

Spencer grins his famous grin. "I'm trying. How am I doing?" As soon as he answers, Myles enters with worry lines creased into his forehead. He sits down at the kitchen table with Mac and Spencer. He asks Spencer if he shared the news, and Spencer shakes his head no.

Mac is wide-eyed. "Okay, guys, what news?"

Myles starts by saying, "David is missing. Someone took him from the backyard sometime this afternoon. George found his lighter. We can only assume the suspect got to him. With security increased, I'm not sure how this happened. We'll set all the alarms along with the motion sensors on the outer perimeter. I've engaged the remote monitoring systems too. We can see the cameras from a computer or a phone."

"Whoa, dad. Do you mean they took David from *our* backyard? Like right out there?" Mac says as she points to the area just beyond the pool.

Myles lowers his head. "I'm afraid so. David walked along the tree line for whatever reason." Myles's cell phone rings, and he jumps up and runs to the back door. He watches George come in from the forest carrying something over his shoulder. Myles opens the back door and yells for Spencer. Myles and Spencer sprint toward George. When they reach him, they realize he's carrying David. Someone knocked David unconscious, and an enormous goose egg formed on the back of his head. Myles dials 911 for an ambulance. They gingerly carry David into the house and lay him on the sofa.

Myles asks David, "Did you recognize who hit you? Did you smell anything? Clothes?"

David tries to sit up, but after his stomach flips, he lays back down. He says there was a noise in the woods, and he walked toward it. When he didn't find a reason for the noise, he turned around to walk back to the house when someone struck him on the back of the head, and he landed hard on the ground. When he came to a little later, the guy was trying to put him over his shoulder. All he remembers is short black hair. Then he passed out again. He knew nothing else until George shook him awake.

Myles is livid, as is Spencer. They paced the floor. Mac has never seen her dad act this way, let alone Spencer. Both are in deep thought. Myles walks while talking on the phone, and Spencer walks around in circles. Circles around Mac.

Mac sticks her hand out and states, "You're making me dizzy. I can't keep watching you walk around me. What is going on? David will be fine, but he'll require a hospital trip."

"I can't figure this one out. I keep saying someone in the agency is causing this havoc, but I can't put the finger on who. They associate none of the task force members to the class with Honeycutt. The person who snatched David is unknown. Short black hair. All of us guys have short hair."

Myles asks, "Has anyone spoken to Stubin yet?" Spencer said he called and left a message on Stubin's cell phone. Myles advises he and George are going back to the woods to see if they can find anything they missed earlier. They'll search fifty yards into the woods and call it quits if they find nothing. Myles has already sent the shoe prints to his lab.

While everyone was together, Spencer shared Honeycutt's warrant information before they left for the woods. Honeycutt doesn't appear to have been in the house for over a month. The house was dark and dirty. Spider webs had set up home in Honeycutt's absence. If Honeycutt skipped out after Burke's murder, he might have been in Daytona all this time.

Mac questions Honeycutt's finances. "Where did he get his money to stay in Daytona all this time? It's not free to stay at the beach. Chastain told us Honeycutt's finances were bleak. Someone helped him get to Daytona Beach."

Myles states they'll consider Mac's questions in a bit, but he wants to survey the woods before they lose daylight. George agrees to a walk in the woods. The culprit somehow entered the backyard unseen. Once Myles and George leave for the woods, Spencer, and Mac are alone. Spencer walks over to Mac and wraps his arms around her. He holds her tight, neither one uttering a word. They enjoy the contact because they need the other. He pulls back and looks into Mac's eyes, and he reads the fear in them. He wants to be the one to keep her safe, but he doesn't know from whom. This mess is driving him nuts. They stare at each other for a minute, and he admits, "I couldn't help myself. I just needed to hold you and touch you. To make sure you are okay."

"I need you, too, desperately. This entire ordeal upsets me." Mac wants to say how much she wants Spencer to hold her, but she can't, not yet. The time isn't right. If she lives through this, she'll tell him. She can't hold it in much longer. She loves this man without a doubt.

Chapter 12

Mac suggests they go upstairs to the office while her dad and George return to the woods. They are heading up the stairs when Mac's mom runs into the house, yelling for Mac. Mac turns and runs down the stairs into the kitchen. Mary witnessed the ambulance pulling out from the driveway and demanded an explanation since she was away at the grocery store. Mac explains the situation with David, and she tells her mom that dad and George are in the woods. Mary calms down enough to go to the kitchen as she insists on keeping busy because all this activity is too much for her heart.

Mac returns to Spencer's side, and he sees the worry around her eyes again. When Spencer sees her like this, it makes him more motivated to find the culprit.

They work on the cards for a while, but they're not leading them in a different direction. Honeycutt must give them valuable information. They depend on him because he's the only one that can help jump-start this case. Maybe he'll keep babbling until Stubin and Baxter get down there to talk with him. Honeycutt has to divulge Seth Campbell's hiding spot. Without Seth's location, they remain at a loss.

Mac asks Spencer, "Wonder what happened to Honeycutt? Did he make it to a class for the FBI? I don't remember anyone saying that, and I don't remember his name on the rosters."

Spencer says, "Let me check and see if I can find out. I don't remember having that in our cards either." Spencer reviews the cards and then his notes. He doesn't find the information either. So why would Honeycutt shoot somebody if it weren't personal? The pieces to the puzzle remained scattered.

Agent Williams calls and requests another update. Mac tells him about the mishap with David. Over the next thirty minutes, Spencer discusses the situation with Williams. They talk through several scenarios, and none of them seem quite right. There is always a little something keeping the scene from playing out to the end.

Spencer asks Williams. "So was Honeycutt, a student in one of the FBI classes? We can't find any information that confirms or denies his attendance."

Williams eases their minds. "Yes. He was. Burke reprimanded him with a few negative comments regarding his ability to shoot long distances. The team working on Burke's murder wants to talk with Honeycutt as soon as possible. They want to get a hold of his weapon for a ballistics comparison."

"Interesting information. Did anyone check the roster of classmates against Honeycutt's class?" Spencer questions.

"Yes, we checked the list. Seth Campbell is not on it. We don't have a connection between Campbell and Honeycutt yet," explains Agent Williams.
Williams says his phone is beeping with a call from Stubin. He quickly tells Spencer he'll call him back as soon as he finishes with Stubin. Spencer turns around and tells Mac that Williams is on a call with Stubin.

Mac sits on the couch with her feet tucked securely under her. She silently prays Stubin has new information because staying cooped up is no fun. Mac watches Spencer speak with her dad and George. She doesn't even want to join the discussion, even though it doesn't appear to be good news. She is numb, but her nerves remain on edge.

Her mom brings her a drink. Mary pleads with Mac, "Please drink this. You have had nothing to eat or drink in hours."

"I'm not hungry, but I am a little thirsty. Thanks, how can you stay sane? This is so hard."

Mary grins at her daughter. "Yes, you're right. Life is hard. But being with your dad for so many years, I've been in terrible predicaments before. We'll survive."

"You always have a brilliant way of making me calm down when I need it. My nerves are going haywire as my world crashes. This is not what I had envisioned when I signed up to work at the FBI."

"I have told you since you were a little girl, you are smart. If anyone can figure out who is doing this, you can. Just use the brains God gave you, and you'll be fine."

"I love you, Mom." Mac hugs her mom and then watches her exit the room.

Spencer takes a seat beside her. "Everything okay? You looked like you were having a deep conversation."

"Yeah, we're fine. Mom hands me stuff to eat and drink all the time, just like always. Food and drink are the answers to making someone feel better. Anything new?"

"I'm waiting for Williams or Stubin to call. Stubin called Williams while I was on the phone with him. I'm dying to hear what Honeycutt told them."

Everyone sits around, each lost in their thoughts when the house alarms sound. Spencer grabs Mac's hand and leads her to the safe room. Then he finds Mary and does the same. Myles runs to the video room while George walks down the hall to the tactical room. Myles has enough firearms to supply a mini-army, and George picks his favorite weapon for home defense: a 410-gauge shotgun. They have a wide shot pattern, so the shooter doesn't have to worry about aiming at their target. He also carries his 40 caliber gun on his waistband and a 380 pocket pistol. After George grabs his shotgun, he trots to the front of the house. He meets Spencer in the hallway, carrying an AR-15, as he checks to make sure the gun safety is off. When he looks up, he's staring into George's face.

"George, why didn't you say something? I didn't hear you walking toward me." Spencer whispered.

"That's the whole point, right? If you're heading to a gun battle, you need to be quiet."
Spencer grimaces. "I suppose. But you still could have said something—quietly!"

Everyone takes up their positions in under thirty seconds. Myles turns off the alarms when he realizes the culprit is a flower delivery boy at the front door. And then Myles says, "Can someone come to the front door? I don't know who or why someone would send flowers here."
George and Spencer walk to the foyer and stand on each side of the door while Myles opens it. The young boy stands on the porch, holding an enormous bouquet.

Myles asks the boy, "What can I do for you?"

The boy replies he has a delivery for MacKenzie Morris. Myles mutters to himself, "MacKenzie." Now, who would send something here with that name on it? He takes the flowers from the kid and sends the boy on his way. Then he marches straight to the control room. He scans the flowers for detonation devices, bugging devices, and anything else that comes to mind. The flowers are safe. Myles takes the vase to the safe room where Mac and Mary are waiting. He opens the door, and both women hug him.

Myles offers the flowers to Mac. "Delivery for one MacKenzie Morris."

Mac stares at him. "No one calls me that. Who sent them?"

"All I did was scan the flowers and make sure they were safe. I didn't read the card. Saved it for you." Myles grinned.

Mac unhooks the card from the plastic holder and opens it slowly. She reads it but doesn't believe it. The card flutters to the floor, and Mac steps back. Spencer sees her reaction and reaches for the card. He reads it but can't believe it either. The card reads, "I'm coming for you!"

Spencer hands the card to Myles, and he reads it while shaking his head. "This is one brazen guy," utters Myles. "How in the world did they track her here? And better yet, why would they try to get to her while she is here? If they know my background, they know we have firearms and refuse to back down to a firefight. Should we move her somewhere else? Keep her moving around for a while?"

"That's a thought, Myles. We have to do something. They've already gotten to David. It doesn't scare them to come after Mac here." Spencer declared.

Myles hands the card to George. All Myles says is, "Dust it." George tries his best to recover fingerprints even though it's a long shot since many people have already touched the card.

Spencer answers a call on his cell from Williams. "Sir. We've just encountered another situation." Spencer continues telling Williams what transpired with the flower delivery.
It takes Williams two seconds before he speaks. "I can't believe this guy. I'm glad all of you are safe. Maybe you should take Myles up on the idea of moving around. Throw it around some more. I like the idea. Stubin called with nothing on Honeycutt. Honeycutt is sober now, and he's

not talking. He wants a boatload of money and an attorney before he will spill his guts, but then he clams up and says he knows nothing. Stubin is working with the judge to get Honeycutt's rifle for a ballistics comparison. They found it in Honeycutt's truck. The sketch from Abby is not a match for Honeycutt. No question on that. Honeycutt is round-faced, blue-eyed, tall, and blond-haired."

Williams adds, "Stubin and Baxter are staying in Florida at least through tomorrow. They will confirm his lodging arrangements. Also, they are trying to get Honeycutt to talk to his cellmate. Honeycutt is unaware his cellmate is an undercover agent for the sheriff's office. Stubin says Honeycutt has shifty eyes, and he gets the impression Honeycutt is holding out on them. Stubin wants to keep trying. He refuses to give up on Honeycutt."

"Good. I don't want them giving up either. If he has information, Stubin and Baxter need to beat it out of him. This guy has turned Mac and her family upside down, along with the other agents. He made this personal now by sending flowers to the house if he is the sender. But the flower sender might be the sidekick, Seth. Who knows what is next?"

Williams pauses for a moment, "I've wondered how desperate this guy is, and I can't figure out his trigger either. Why has the suspect gone to this much trouble to get to Mac? Why Mac? We can't find anyone in her class that matches the suspect's description nor the two classes before hers. Honeycutt was in class but not with a guy named Seth Campbell, and his class was a long time ago. No one can tell us the connection. I'll check in with Reagan and ask if she can explain the flower delivery significance."

"Thanks." Spencer walks around the room. Then he mutters to himself, "I bet the guy didn't know if Mac was here or not. He sent the flowers to see if she was here. I'm afraid he'll move faster now. I better share this with Myles." Spencer trots to the control room.

Mac and Myles review roster names of past classes as Spencer shares his thoughts about the flower delivery. Myles agrees and says it makes sense.

"We need to sit down and make a plan. If we must, we can move every couple of days. We can use I^2 for transport if the need arises. I'll check on our safe houses, too, but our houses might be unavailable because of upcoming trials. It seems there is someone at the FBI that has a little too much information."

Mac answers her cell phone, and relief washes over her when Williams is on the line.

"How are you?" he asks Mac.

"OK, I guess, but I've been better if you want to know the truth. I'm ready to get out into the world. Any news?" Williams hesitates. "Sorry, but you're on lockdown for a little while longer. It aggravates the other graduates too. They're calling and sending emails requesting the status of things. Everyone is on edge. I'm calling because I need your help. Baxter just sent the preliminary results on the bullet from Honeycutt's gun. Can I send it to you? I want your eyes on it to see if you can place it at any of the murders."

"It would be an honor, sir. I'll need the other reports as well. They're on my desktop at work. The tech guys are emailing my files to Spencer, but I haven't received them yet. We left in such a hurry I never followed up with them. Can you get the tech guys to set it up so I can access my desktop from here?"

"Yes, that's no problem. We'll assign you a laptop once we capture this guy. I'm unsure what's going on in the lab, but they should have no problem sending you the information," says Williams. "Be on the lookout for it. And call me as soon as you can."
"Sure will, and thanks, Williams."

Mac searches for Spencer and her dad. She finds them sitting around the table with George discussing a plan for her life. She feels a little awkward being left out of the conversation, but they mean well, and at this point, any decision they make, she'll go along with it.
Spencer speaks first. "So, what do you know that we don't?"

"Is it obvious? I just hung up with Williams. He's sending the ballistics from Honeycutt's gun to me. He asked that I compare this bullet to the rest of the murders. I'm happy to have something useful to do. The tech guys are sending me the info so that I can access my desktop. This way, I'll have access to all of my files."

"Sounds great. I'll set you up in the control room. Oh, we never finished the rosters. We need to finish going over the prior classes," says Myles.

Spencer adds, "I can help."

Forty-five minutes later, Mac sits in front of a computer with multiple screens. First, Mac takes the image of Honeycutt's bullet and completes her markings. She notes the grooves and the rifling around the entire spent cartridge.

This is meticulous work, but she does it again and again. She must mark everything, leaving nothing to chance or carelessness. Mac remains locked away in the control room for hours. Spencer comes calling when supper is ready.

Rubbing her eyes, Mac says, "Supper already? This lab stuff is time-consuming. I have more to complete, and then I can start the comparisons."

"Not until you eat. You skipped lunch, remember?" Spencer pointed out.

"I guess I did. I am kind of hungry. Let's go," Mac replies. Then she strolls down the hall toward the kitchen, holding Spencer's hand.

Supper is pleasant as they enjoy talking about anything but the murders. Mac is eager to work on her bullets, so she excuses herself and heads to the control room, leaving the group at the table. She sits down at the desk and takes a deep breath. She believes this will help the case, but she is unsure of how. Mac digs in and starts comparing each groove and landing on each bullet with great precision. At 2335, she finally has a match. Mac calls for her dad and Spencer. The hour is late, but she can't contain her excitement. Myles and Spencer run to the control room. Mac shows the side-by-side comparison of the bullets and each mark on both casings for Myles and Spencer. An hour later, they confirmed the match.

Mac is so relieved she feels like crying. Spencer calls Agent Williams with the update.
"Sorry to call at such a late hour, sir, but we have a ballistic match. The Honeycutt bullet matches the bullet from Burke's murder. We can put Honeycutt at the scene. We

need to tell Stubin and Baxter to grab him. However, there is no match with any of the other shootings."

"Are you sure it matches the Burke murder? I need to be nincty-nine point nine percent sure. Mac is good, but she also wants out of lockdown."

Spencer explains, "Yes. Myles and I sat with her for over an hour, going over each groove and rifling. We have an exact match."

"OK. Keep the info to yourself. We still haven't identified who's on the inside. I'll call Stubin and Baxter and start the process to bring him home since our guys are already there. Impressive job, guys!" Williams disconnects.

Spencer tells Mac and Myles what Williams said. Myles tells them he's going back to bed. They have decisions to make tomorrow, and he suggests they try to sleep too.

Mac and Spencer go downstairs to the kitchen to get something to drink and try to wind down after the excitement. Then they talk, and they don't stop until 0200. Mac loves talking with Spencer. Those eyes of his melt her to her core. The emotional stirrings deep down are new to her. He even gives her a hug and a kiss as they make their way to their respective rooms. When Mac climbs into bed, she realizes how much she wants to be with Spencer. She has never had time for a genuine relationship with a man. Yes, she dated in the past but never anything serious.

She was always in school or trying to beat her brothers in sports. This ordeal has shown her time waits for no one. If you see something you want, you need to go after it before time takes it away. Did she want Spencer? She had never admitted to herself that she needed or wanted anyone. She wondered why these thoughts were coming forth. Perhaps she was tired—tired of working at the computer, tired of being locked up, just plain tired. Mac drifts into a restless sleep, dreaming of her and Spencer.

Stubin and Baxter arrived at the Volusia County Sheriff's Office at 0800 the following day. They met with the Sheriff and produced their arrest warrant and the extradition papers because they wanted Honeycutt on the murder of Special Agent Burke. The sheriff accepted the documents and advised the agents they would process them as soon as possible.

Stubin and Baxter leave the sheriff's office and call Agent Williams. "We've turned the request over to the sheriff and are awaiting instructions. Any idea how long it will take to get Honeycutt released to us?"

Williams replies, "I placed a call myself to the sheriff. He's already working on the paperwork, so I would say within the next two hours. Go have brunch somewhere and then check in with the sheriff again. Honeycutt should be ready for transport."

Mac strolls into the kitchen to see that everyone is already wide awake after a nice large breakfast. She heads straight for the coffee. Spencer has already spoken with Williams, and he gives her the rundown of the extradition papers. They are once again in wait mode. She is sick and tired of wait mode. After breakfast, she heads up to the office to review the rosters yet again. She expresses her disappointment about the ballistics not matching the other murders. However, the one matching Honeycutt with Burke is something. At least they can push one case to the closed side.

Myles asks Spencer, "Are you up for making phone calls today? I'd like to work on our list of Seth Campbell's."

"Yes, I can," Spencer replies. They head to the office with cups of coffee in hand.
The men set up on the other end of the office from Mac. Since they'll be making calls, they don't want to interrupt her. But the calls turn out to be a time-waster. After a few hours pass with nothing to report, the men sit back in their chairs. Myles rubs his temples while Spencer rubs his neck. They turn to face Mac.

Mac studies her computer, searching for anything in the rosters. She's been sitting there for hours, and her eyes are crossing. She places her head in her hands and rubs her temples. Why haven't they found a connection in these rosters? It makes little sense. He has to be there. Was Seth a middle name? First name? Hold on—what about a nickname? She turns around in her seat so fast she almost spins herself right out of it. "Hey, guys. Is Seth a middle name or first name?"
"What? I never thought of that. They gave us the name Seth Campbell, and we've been searching for Seth Campbell," answers Spencer as he glances at Myles.

Myles states, "I hate to say this, but we need to start over with the rosters. Did we notice any other Seth's on the roster? Somebody call Williams and ask if we can get the roster with the middle names included. That might help."

"Mac, you may be on to something. Keep digging."

George calls on the intercom to say that he has a situation and needs reinforcement. Everyone jumps up and runs for the control room.

George points out the black sedan that has been sitting across the street from the house. "The driver is in place and appears to be alone. After an hour, he drives around for a while and comes back to the same spot. I can't get the camera tilted to the right spot to read the tag number, and I can't see the driver's face. The distance is too great. I suggest we check him out, but, Myles, this is your call."

Myles pauses a minute and then says, "I think it's time for a chat. Grab your gear."
Spencer, George, and Myles grab their guns and bulletproof vests and head out the door. Mac stands by and watches as the black Suburban drives slowly down the driveway. They wouldn't even let her drive the truck. She doesn't enjoy watching the action unfold from a distance. Spencer exits the truck with his handgun pointed at the driver, screaming for him to exit the vehicle when it speeds off. George follows the sedan, leaving Spencer standing in the road. The sedan rounds the curve and swerves into oncoming traffic with tires screeching.
Myles says as calmly as possible, "Stop him, George. He'll kill somebody."

All George utters is "ten-four." George catches up to the sedan and attempts a pit maneuver. He strikes the car in the right rear quarter panel, hoping the car will go right into the ditch. The driver notices the trick and avoids any significant impact from the collision, but this move sends George and Myles headfirst into a ditch.

Chapter 13

Two minutes later, Spencer runs up to the scene after hearing the crash, finding George knocked out cold. Myles stands beside the crashed SUV, staring at it. The front end takes a direct hit and caves inward. Smoke pours out from under the hood, and shattered glass rests in George's lap where his head struck the window. The windshield remains intact but is spider-webbed with cracks. Spencer sprints to the driver's side to check on George. Blood gushes from a huge gash that extends from his hairline almost to his ear. Spencer grabs a wad of paper towels he finds in the back seat of the Suburban and applies pressure to the wound. George moans with the pressure but refuses to open his eyes. Spencer yells at Myles to come around to his side of the truck.

Myles replies as he sounds woozy, "Here I am. How can I help?"

Spencer glances over his shoulder and sees Myles standing there. "Myles, George is bleeding something awful. Call 911. We need to get him to the ER pronto. If I had to guess, he might have a concussion or something worse from the looks of this head injury. His eyes are glassy, and he most certainly will need stitches to close this wound."

Spencer shifts his body to get a better angle on George's head. With the continuous blood flow, Spencer worries George will bleed out before the emergency crews arrive. He searches the SUV for something to tie around George's head. The only thing he sees is the seatbelt. Spencer shifts his body enough that he cuts the seatbelt free. George tries to move while Spencer ties the seatbelt around his head. Even doing this, the blood flow doesn't stop. Now, it seeps through the paper towels.

Myles dials 911 and explains their location. Three minutes later, patrol cars, EMTs, and a fire truck arrive at the scene. The EMTs take over George's care. They give Spencer a high five for applying pressure with the seatbelt idea. The lead EMT explains head wounds bleed more than most, so the pressure probably saved his life. George's vitals are low, which is understandable due to the blood loss. But his eyes are light reactive. So the EMTs are optimistic George will be fine.

With sirens approaching the house, Mac can't sit back and wait for news. Mac and Mary decide to find the scene of the accident and check it out. Mac retrieves the keys for her car, and they turn left out of the driveway. Within five hundred yards, they arrive at the wreck site. It scares Mac to death. She can't tell who's sitting in the car, and she surmises someone is injured because EMTs surround them as they load the person onto a backboard for transport. She walks around the car and spots Spencer.

Spencer sees her, but he doesn't recognize her right off. When it registers that Mac is standing in front of him, he walks over and says, "What are you doing here? You need to get back to the house. We are unsure if the suspect is still here!"

"We couldn't stand by and wait to find out if all of you were still living or not! Mom wants to check on dad too. I'm sorry if you are mad, but I couldn't wait." Mac turns and stomps off toward her dad. Myles smiles as he watches her approach.

"Mac, can you take your mom home? The accident will tie us up for a little while. We'll come home as soon as we can. George is going to the hospital, and I want to make sure he will be okay."

"I'll take Mom home, but please call me if anything changes with George's condition." Mac turns to Mary, "Come on, Mom. Let's go. No one needs us here."

Mac takes her mom's hand, and they head for her car. When Mac places her hand on the car door handle to open it, she notices a black sedan driving slowly by the accident scene.

Spencer yells, "Mac, get down!"

Mac stares at the car as the driver points his thumb and index finger at her like a gun. And she falters as she climbs into the car. Spencer runs over to Mac's car before she closes the door.

"Did you recognize the driver?" Spencer asks Mac.

Mac shakes her head no. "I didn't get a good look at his face. I was too busy concentrating on the fake gun pointed at me!" Mac slams the door and heads for the house.

Mac and her mom return home, and Mac heads straight for the office. She vaguely recognized the driver with dark hair and dark eyes. She goes directly to the sketch. Mac sucks in a breath when she sees the sketch. It's the same person! She knows it! Now how can I put a name to this person? Mac tries not to question herself, but she can't help it. She hasn't been sleeping well because she ponders about her life with Spencer and the killer lurking around. Her emotions are in complete turmoil. Although, after the meeting at the accident, Spencer may not want to be with her anymore because he seemed to be genuinely mad that she went to the scene.

"Well, he can just be mad!" Mac tells herself. "I'm tired of waiting around. I'm ready to be back at the office. The killer has my location now. I'll talk to dad about relocating since I don't want him or mom to be in danger because of me."

Mac sits at the desk and notices mail lying to the side. She flips through it and finds a letter addressed to her but without a return address. She contemplates this when noises come from downstairs. Before going down the stairs, she draws her service weapon. The sounds lessen as she creeps down the stairs, but she continues with her gun drawn as she rounds the corner. Then she realizes she is pointing it at Spencer.

Spencer sidesteps to the right and says, "Whoa, now. You can lower your weapon. Myles went with George to the hospital. I'll pick them up soon."

Mac says sheepishly, "Sorry, I guess I'm a little jumpy."

Spencer reaches for Mac and pulls her in a big old bear hug. Then he kisses her—a slow, inviting kiss. Mac relaxes as she lays her head on his shoulder, soaking up his strength. She can't believe how calming it is for Spencer to wrap his arms around her.

"I'm sorry I acted like a jerk. First, George's injuries worried me, then you showed up at the scene followed by the idiot in the car, and I almost lost my mind." Spencer runs his hands up and down Mac's upper arm.

"I didn't think you cared anymore. You just stared at me when you saw me. I at least thought you would come over and tell me what happened."

"I should have, and I apologize. Please forgive me?" Spencer pleads.

Mac waits for a heartbeat before she replies. "You keep giving hugs and kisses like this, and I'll forgive you."

Spencer and Mac share a moment. They have a mutual attraction, but they realize things are on hold between this investigation and their jobs.

Mac straightens herself and turns toward the refrigerator. She reaches in and grabs bottled water as she tries to calm the emotions running between them.

"Oh, I need to show you something in the office. I just found a piece of mail addressed to me without a return address on it."

"When did you get it?" Lines crease Spencer's forehead.

"I can't say how long it has been here. I found it in the office while I compared the sketch with the car driver I saw."

"Did the sketch match?"

"Yes, I believe so. I want to ID this guy so bad I can't stand it."

"Let's go read the letter." Offered Spencer.

Spencer and Mac walk to the office hand in hand, and Mac walks over to the desk, then hands the letter to Spencer. "Here. See what I mean? No return address."

Spencer takes the envelope in his hand with a tissue, not wanting to add additional fingerprints to the envelope. He takes care of opening the envelope and eases out the letter. He reads it before showing it to Mac. She'll have a hard time with this one. Spencer places the letter down on the desk so it's visible to Mac. The letter is on a standard piece of white paper. Nothing extraordinary about the paper itself. It appears to be a typical white printer paper. The letter says is, "Your time is coming! Are you ready?"

The sender prints the words in black block font. Anyone could have typed it on a PC.

Mac states, "I can't believe this. More threats. Are any of the other agents getting threats like this? Why me?"

"I still can't answer that. However, I suggest we move. We can't take the chance of staying here. I want to speak to your dad when he gets back from the hospital with George. Myles called someone else, Luke, I think, to give them a ride home. He wants me to stay here because he's already lost, two guys. We might need to bring in agency guys for reinforcement."

"Who can we trust? I thought we decided someone on the inside is part of this murder scheme." Mac questions while her head swings from side to side.

Spencer thinks for a second. "I still agree. There is no way anyone knows where you are except someone on the inside, but we still need some of our guys. Your dad is low on investigators because of the trial that's going on, so we might have to use our agency personnel."

"If that is true, then let them come and get me. I'm tired of the wait! Let's work up a plan to use me to bring them out in the open. Once we get them out, we capture them."

Spencer's eyebrows draw together. "I don't like using you as bait. You would be in a dangerous situation. Surely we can come up with another plan."

It frustrates Mac. She glares at Spencer and says, "Whatever." Then she stalks off to the bathroom and slams the door shut.

Spencer's phone vibrates in his pocket. He doesn't even want to answer it. He wills it to go away. Locked in the bathroom, Mac is mad at him, and he needs to talk to her. He doesn't need another distraction, and he can't leave this conversation unfinished. The phone continues vibrating, so he fishes it out and looks at the caller ID flashing Agent Williams.

Agent Williams sounds out of breath. "We have a situation at the safe house in Ellijay. Can you get there as soon as possible?"

"Yeah, sure. What's wrong? Didn't they just move in there a few days ago?" Spencer asks.

"Someone fired shots into the house fifteen minutes ago. We have no idea about injuries yet. Cell phone coverage is scarce at this location, and the weather is stormy there, which is not helping anything. I need your eyes on it. Oh— how is George?"

Spencer replies, "We've received no updates on George's condition. Myles hasn't made it home yet from the hospital. I can leave now, but Mac will be alone. She is so angry at the world. She received a threatening letter in the mail. I want to have it analyzed for fingerprints and DNA. Perhaps the guy licked the envelope. I'll call as soon as I get to the Ellijay. Best I can figure, I am around an hour away without lights."

Williams spoke sternly, "Use the lights." Then he disconnects the call.

Spencer walks to the bathroom and speaks to Mac through the door about the Ellijay situation. He hears nothing, but he knows she's there. When he says he must leave and go to the safe house in Ellijay, Mac slowly cracks open the door with tears glistening in her eyes. He reaches into the bathroom and pulls her out of the doorway and right into his arms.

He calmly tells her, "Mac, don't cry. We'll get this guy. He's getting sloppy now. He just shot a safe house with FBI agents inside and didn't hit a soul. A few more days, and this will be over. I'll be back as soon as I can. But I want you to stay put. Can you do that for me?" Spencer pleads.

Mac doesn't speak for fear a tear will escape. She just nods her head. Spencer leaves the house with Mac watching from the top of the stairs. Mac feels vulnerable in this enormous house with only her mom. Yes, her mom can shoot guns, but her nerves are not the greatest under this much pressure. Mac wanders around the house, making sure they lock the doors. On her rounds, she finds Mary in the laundry room.

Mary states to Mac, "You seem out of sorts today."

"I'm okay, tired of this crazy mess. Wondering if I should pick a different line of work after all." Mac walks over to the window and peeks through the blinds.

"Oh, come on now, Mac. There is no comparison between the murders and the line of work. Someone just has a grudge against the FBI, which is the only way they know how to right a wrong. You've wanted to be an FBI agent for years now. Don't give it up just yet."

"What did you say, Mom? Go back to the part about righting a wrong. What made you say that?"

"I'm not sure. It sounds logical. Whoever is doing this thinks their actions are setting things right. I can't answer what happened to them in the past or why."

"Interesting," Mac continues, "Mom, stay inside. We're alone. I'll let the dogs inside until someone gets here with us. Spencer went to Ellijay to the safe house. Someone just used the house for target practice. He'll return as soon as possible. Is there any word from dad yet?"

"Yes. He should be home soon. George received fifty stitches in his head and has a mild concussion. Dad is bringing him home. We'll have to watch George overnight and make sure he wakes up on the hour for a while. Other than that, he should be fine in a day or two. He got lucky on this one. He looked awful with blood pouring out of his forehead."

"That's the best news I've heard in a long time. I'll be glad to have George and dad home."

Mac walks upstairs to the office. She rehashes what her mom said about righting a wrong. What happened that someone would consider it wrong? Someone in the FBI academy that didn't make it, we've already worked that idea. What else? There isn't anything else that would involve the agency. Where are those rosters? It has to be in there. Somehow, the name is unique. Mac tells herself to go back to the rosters and start from the beginning. She reads through the class names before Honeycutt's class. Nothing registers—no Seth on the list. Wait! She jumps up and grabs her cell phone. She dials Williams. He answers on the first ring.

"Hi, Agent Williams. I realize you're busy with the Ellijay house, but I wondered if you received the rosters with the middle names yet. I want to go through them and see if they list any Seth's."

Agent Williams clicks keys on his desktop. "It's here. The email came in this morning, but I just checked when you called. I'm sending it over now. Send me updates as you receive them. I need to run. Talk soon."

"OK, no problem," Mac says to a dead phone.

As soon as the call ends with Agent Williams, Spencer calls. "You wouldn't believe this house. Bullet holes cover the entire front wall. I'm bringing you a present. There are so many shell casings littering the road that I took one after the crime lab tech photographed it. I want to know if it matches any of the other ones. Thankfully, none of the agents were shot. We had two agents that required medical attention because of flying glass as they leaped for cover. The culprit got all the windows on the front of the house and most of the siding. The house will get a complete face-lift. We're moving the agents now to another house in a neighboring county. I should be back there with you in two hours."

"Okay. Good. Agent Williams just sent me the new rosters with the full names of the class attendees. I'll compare them because I'm determined to find something. The answer is in the rosters somewhere. I just haven't found it yet."

"We'll work on it when I return." Spencer offers.

"Be safe," states Mac and as she disconnects the call, the garage door opens. She flies down the back stairs to see who arrived. She enters the kitchen and finds her dad and George. George appears to have been beaten by an entire gang of people.

"Oh, George. Your head. Your eye. It looks so painful," said Mac wrinkling her nose.

George smirks a little and says, "It's not as bad as it looks except for being woozy. That makes me nauseous, and I don't like being nauseous."

Mary adds, "Anybody hungry? I have supper ready."

George peeks at the stove and turns an unnatural green color right there in the middle of the kitchen. He shakes his head.

Mac laughs and adds, "I don't think George is up for eating yet. You better lie down, George. We'll check on you in a little while."

Myles walks over to the sink and washes his hands. "I'm famished. Let's eat! Where is Spencer?" Myles escorts the pups to their room so they can eat too.

Mac explains all that transpired while he was away, starting with the shooting in Ellijay and ending with the letter. Myles is silent. He mulls over all the information he received. Then he says, "Where is the envelope? I want to run fingerprints and try to get DNA off of it."

"Spencer said you would, and we have it on the desk. I touched the envelope but not the letter. Spencer hopes the idiot licked the envelope and left DNA."

"I'll process this one myself. Was it mailed to the house or delivered?"

Mac replies, "They mailed the letter to the Atlanta office, then forwarded to me at the house."

"Good. We can find out the post office they mailed it from and check if they have surveillance cameras. We might get lucky, and the person at the counter might remember this letter if they mailed it from the inside. Our luck, he mailed it using a drop box."

Myles ventures to the lab after supper and begins processing the letter and envelope. A little while later, Spencer arrives, making his way to the lab to join Myles. He wants to discuss moving Mac to a safe house of his choosing. Spencer used the house for a witness about four months ago and hasn't used it since. The home sits in a remote setting in Walker County. The mountains are high, and the roads steep. It would be easier to keep a watch over Mac if she were in the house up there.

153

"Myles, I want to discuss moving Mac to a new location."
Spencer shares the details about the safe house and the
security it offers.

"I'm not sure I believe you are the only one familiar with
this safe house. I don't know, Spencer. This entire thing
screams weird to me. They figured out she was here, so I
think they can find her anywhere."

"I guarantee only two people have any knowledge of this
house in Walker County. I used it to protect a prosecution
witness against a drug kingpin because dangerous things
kept happening to the people around the case. Once I
accepted the assignment, I found the safe house. Then, I
rented it in a fake name and paid in cash for a six-month
lease. Agent Williams knows nothing about this one. So,
only me and my witness know of this house."

"Well, if that's the case, then it might work. We'll discuss
this with Mac, I guess. I'm unsure how she will react."

Spencer agrees, and he heads to the office.

Spencer walks in, and Mac is bent over the desk studying
something. He taps her shoulder, and Mac jumps out of the
chair, knocking it over.

"Easy does it. I didn't mean to scare you. I figured you
heard me when I entered," said Spencer as he reached for
her hand.

"You must have been quiet, or I guess I was too deep in
thought when you came into the office." Mac lifts her chair
back to its wheels.

"Your dad and I would like to discuss something with you. Would you mind walking down to the lab with me? Your dad is up to his elbows, processing the letter and the envelope."

"Sure. What is it? Please tell me there's been no other shootings?"

"No. No. Nothing like that. Just something we would like you to consider." Spencer takes her by the hand and leads her to the lab.

When they reach the lab, Myles is studying fingerprints. "I have a partial print. It might be a thumbprint. I got it off the envelope. I haven't gotten to the letter yet. So, Mac, sit down for a second. Spencer has something to say."

It shocks Spencer when Myles turns it over to him to sell the idea to Mac to move her to a safe house in the mountains. Spencer squirms in his chair, trying to come up with the right words. Although she mentioned it earlier, is she still open to it? Myles is her safety net and always will be.

"Out with it, Spencer. No sugar coating. Please!" Mac exclaims.

Spencer clears his throat and begins his sales pitch. "Mac, I would like you to consider moving to a safe house in Walker County. The house is secure because I rented it in a fake name and paid cash for it for six months. It would be for your safety. Of course, I will go along too."

"You want me to leave here and go stay someplace in the mountains? I'm unfamiliar with the territory up there.

Before, when I mentioned it, I thought I would be with other agents."

Spencer continues talking. "Number one, I'll be there, and I'll always have your back. Number two, the location is remote. The killer will have to follow us to find it."

Mac looks at her dad, and Myles shrugs his shoulders, knowing how torn up inside Mac is over this whole situation. She struggles with the decision.

"Mac, only you can decide. You said you wanted to get away from here to protect your mom. Now is your chance." Myles adds.

"Can I at least process the shell casing Spencer brought back from the latest shooting in Ellijay?"

"Well, yes. Process away," says Myles, as he turns back to continue his lab work. Myles doesn't want her leaving his house, but he understands Spencer's thinking. Myles truly feels Spencer will protect his only daughter until his death. He continues his work with a knot in his throat the size of a baseball.

Chapter 14

Several hours later, Mac exclaims, "I have a match! I have a match! I can, without a doubt, match the shooter at this latest gun battle to Fran Evans's shooting. Both bullets are 223 rifle rounds. The grooves and the landings match."

Spencer and Mac grin from ear to ear, and they celebrate with a hug and kiss. When they realize what they've done, they gaze at each other. Mac thinks it odd how comfortable she is with Spencer. Something good happens, and she turns to Spencer.

Spencer speaks first. "I knew you would link these shootings together. Call Agent Williams as this will cheer him up now that there is a link."

Mac walks over to the desk to retrieve her cell phone when it rings. She turns a ghastly pale color and freezes. Myles jumps up out of his chair and reaches for the phone. He checks the caller ID. "Restricted caller" blinks on the ID screen. He shows it to Spencer.

Spencer says, "Unbelievable." Spencer guides Mac over to the chair and eases her into it. Her brain is foggy for a few seconds. Then the color returns to her face. Myles hooks the phone to the digital dialer they have in the lab. He works on the computer keyboard for a few strokes, and then it flashes up on the screen. All eyes grow wide because no one believes it. The call is coming from the area surrounding the FBI headquarters in Atlanta.

Spencer uses his phone to contact Agent Williams, but Agent Williams is unavailable, and his call flows into his voice mail. Spencer ends the call and tries again. Same thing. Voice mail answers. He gives up and dials Drake because he wants the names of anyone in the building.

Drake answers and Spencer explains their situation.

Drake stammers and replies, "Wow. Someone in this building. I thought it was just a few of us working tonight. Let me walk around and see who I find. Talk to me while I walk. What's been going on? Agent Williams has shared a little with us. Is George going to be OK?"

Spencer tries to make small talk, but it's hard. He wants answers on who's in the building, and he wants them now! "Yes, George will be fine. He has many stitches, lost a lot of blood, and has a mild concussion. George will be out of work for several days, but David is back. He is taking George's place at the moment. Myles's cases are piling up since he is running short on guys."

"If Myles needs help, let me know. I'll help any way I can."

"Okay, I'll tell him. We're moving Mac to a safe house in the next couple of days. Have you found anybody in the office yet?"

"Still walking and talking. I ran into a few cleaning people. Agent Williams is still here. Lacey is here. Not sure about anyone on any of the other floors."
"Thanks for checking. If you see anyone unfamiliar, will you check them out for me? They're calling Mac's phone, but it says restricted caller. Thanks, Drake."

Spencer updates Myles and Mac on his conversation with Drake. Then he considers the caller might be in the parking lot, and if that is so, Spencer has no way of locating them.

Myles asks, "Did you call anyone else to confirm what Drake told you? I thought we had Drake under suspicion." Myles shifts in his seat and spots the information on the envelope. He continues, "someone mailed the envelope from a post box in downtown Atlanta. I'm searching for a camera, but I'm not holding out hope."

"No, I didn't confirm Drake's statement. I didn't realize I needed to, but I should have, and yes, Mac has questioned Drake's intentions from the beginning."

"I wouldn't trust anyone at headquarters. I hate to admit it, but it's true," states Myles.

"You're right. How many people have this phone number? It isn't even one of ours," Spencer points out.

Mac suggests, "Spencer, call Stubin. If he's there, ask him to confirm Drake's information." Mac paces while Spencer places the next call.

Spencer taps his speed dial list and hits the button for Stubin. On the third ring, Stubin answers. "Stubin."

"This is Spencer. Can you check our floor and tell me who's working tonight? Don't ask why. Just give me a rundown of the people there, please. I'll explain later."

"Okay. Hold your horses. I'm in the break room, grabbing coffee. We were planning on hitting the rosters tonight. We eliminated the remaining Seth Campbell's on the list."

"Great. More good news. Can it get any better than this?"

"Calm down, Spencer. We'll find this guy and put an end to this! I'm starting my parade of one, and I see Drake sitting at his desk, typing something into his computer. Cameron is here reading. Agent Williams is on the phone in his office, and there is Lacey. I can't tell what she is doing. That is all I see. Now can you tell me what this is about?"

Spencer explains what happened. Stubin interjects by saying, "That could have been any of us. This building is extensive, Spencer, and the caller might be in the parking lot."

"I realize that, but her dad's PI firm registered the phone Mac is using, not the agency. So it has to be someone close to the investigation for them to have her info."

Stubin thinks for a minute. "That sketch from the girl in Athens, did you compare it to the agents in the Atlanta field office?"
"No, we didn't, but we need it too! Thanks, Stubin. I'll let you know when we have an answer. I'm asking Myles to run the comparisons in his lab. You should see this place. Talk about bells and whistles. I wish we had one at headquarters."

They disconnect their call. Spencer turns around, and Mac stands, leaning against the wall. She appears all better now with her rosy cheeks and her perfect hair. It lies on her shoulders where he wants his hands to be. Her lips are smooth and shiny. He walks over to her and hugs her. Mac asks Spencer, "So what's the plan?"

Spencer replies, "Stubin had an outstanding idea. He suggested we compare Abby's sketch against active FBI agents in the Atlanta field office. We might get lucky."

"Or we might get in trouble. We can't go around running comparisons like that without other agents finding out. So, no, I can't agree with it."

"Hey, slow down while I explain. If the FBI lab runs them, everyone will know. We'll use your dad's, and we'll be the only ones that know it—other than Stubin, but he suggested it."

"I guess it would be okay as long as dad has the time. He told mom he had to travel to Orlando for a case. The court case will last for at least a week. I'm hoping he can put off the trip until we capture the gunman."

"I'll ask if he has the time to start it now. Then, if he gets it started, I can finish it."

Mac walks into the kitchen, where her mom and dad stop talking. "Am I interrupting anything, or were you talking about me?"

"A little of both," answers Myles. "We were discussing your move to Spencer's safe house. Of course, your mom and I want you here even though we are all sitting ducks since they have already tried to reach you while you were here. But I don't want them trying again and succeeding, and I don't want Mary in the crossfire."

"I understand, and I still haven't decided. We're still working on a plan. But, dad, we need your help again. Stubin suggested we run Abby's sketch against all the active and inactive agents in the Atlanta field office."

"I like the idea. However, it will take time to get set up, and I'm scheduled for a conference call in fifteen minutes. So as soon as I am done with it, we'll move to the comparisons."

"Great. I'll share with Spencer. We're going back over the rosters because something is missing. Come get us when the conference call is over."

Mac exits the kitchen, knowing full well her parents will continue their discussion on the situation. She hates putting them in this predicament, especially her mom, because her mom worries all the time about her, anyway. This type of situation doesn't help with the concerns.
Back in the office, Mac explains the situation to Spencer. He's excited about the comparisons, and he hopes they will find something because they can use a celebration. He can't keep his eyes off of her. Here she is walking around in blue jeans and an untucked button-up shirt and no makeup, and she is gorgeous. He loves the way those green eyes sparkle with gold flakes when she realizes she has something. Her entire face comes alive. Spencer recognizes he must keep her alive long enough to celebrate. If she is injured or killed, he wouldn't be able to live with himself. How could he wake up every day knowing he let her down? Let her parents down? He can't bear the thought! He shakes his head, trying to clear the most disturbing reflections from his mind.

Mac watches him go through this myriad of emotions and says, "What are you thinking, Spencer? You look troubled."

He looks deep into her eyes before he replies, "Everything. That's all I can say right now. One day, we'll sit and just talk, and I'll share with you, but right now, we have more important items on our list, and we need to get started."

Spencer turns and tries to walk away when Mac grabs his arm. "Promise me we'll sit and just talk one day. I want to hear your story. All of it."

Spencer grins that most excellent way of his as he heads for the desk, and Mac's heart melts all over again.

Mac and Spencer sit together in silence for a little while. Both act like they're going through the rosters—with neither one seeing anything on the papers. Mac's brain travels from the rosters to Spencer and back again. She can't keep her concentration even though the rosters hold a clue. But where?

Mac breaks the silence. "Could one of these names be a different version?"

Spencer's forehead creases as he asks, "What are you talking about?"

"Let me show you. Here. Look at this name. James Campbellton." Mac highlights the name.

"Okay. I see it. So?"

Mac sighs. "We're searching for Seth Campbell, remember. Could James Campbellton be Seth Campbell to Honeycutt?"

"That's a thought. But James Campbellton doesn't have a middle name listed on the roster. I wonder why. Let me call Agent Williams. See if he can find out for us." Spencer dials Agent Williams, and he answers quickly.

"Spencer, I hope you have good news. Drake and Lacey are sitting here with me."

"We have a question for you. There's a name on a roster that doesn't have a middle name listed. Can you request a list with middle names included for this class? Our original request included none for this roster."

"I believe I can. What name and what class?" asks Williams.

"The name is James Campbellton. He was in the FBI academy two classes before Honeycutt. This roster is older than the others, and we're not sure if this is our guy, but Mac wants to check him out. She says the names are too close."

"I agree with Mac. This guy could use an alias with Honeycutt. Call me as soon as you find something."

Spencer disconnects, then turns to Mac and tells her about Drake and Lacey being in the office with Williams. He emphasizes Drake heard the conversation about James Campbellton.

"So why is there a strange look on your face? Are you concerned with him being there?"

Spencer is quiet for a moment, and then he states, "I hope I wasn't wrong about Drake. He sure is close to Agent Williams, and Drake has never acted like that before. He's usually a little standoffish to the bosses. Now he seems to always be around Williams somehow."

"Oh, so now you are questioning Drake? I've said the whole time he's awkward. I can't put my finger on it, but he gives me the creeps. However, he doesn't strike me as someone who would kill agents. He's been with the agency for a long time. So what is his motivation for killing recent graduates? That makes little sense. Doesn't it?"

Mac wants a reply. When she doesn't get one, she walks around to look him in the face. Spencer is concentrating. She gives him his space. Later, Spencer comes over to her side of the office.

"I sure hope this isn't Drake because that means I've helped him along the way. I don't know how I'll handle it if it turns out to be him. Somebody will have to hold me back from killing him myself!"

Spencer's words shock Mac. She's never witnessed an outburst from him. She doesn't have a response, so she shakes her head and pretends to reread the rosters.

Mac's phone rings again, but she is prepared this time. She opens it and says hello. Of course, there is nothing more than heavy breathing. But there are sounds this time, and she concentrates on them, but it's so irritating. To hear something and not be able to describe, is frustrating. There it is again. It's sirens in the background. They're getting louder and louder, which means they are getting closer. Wait, a second—Mac points out the window to Spencer. She jots a message on paper, telling him to look out the front of the house. Spencer sprints to the window, but he sees nothing. He waves at her that he is going downstairs. Mac tries to get the caller to talk, but they never reply. After two minutes, they disconnect.
Mac flies down the stairs, hoping Spencer finds someone waiting in a car. But, unfortunately, by the time she reaches the bottom floor, Spencer is nowhere in sight.

"Please let him be safe. No more death" prays Mac. She yells for her dad, but no one answers her cries. She can't believe they left her alone. Mac runs from window to window, looking outside just to catch of glimpse of something, anything. Mary runs into the room, searching for Mac, and Mac runs into her mother's arm. Mary tries to console her, but she's never seen her daughter like this before. In time, Mac calms down enough to ask about the others.

Mary explains, "Myles left with Spencer as soon as the commotion began. Neither Myles nor Spencer have checked in yet, but David is upstairs in the office, monitoring the radios. Myles left on the ATV from the back barn, and Spencer ran the other way on foot. With any luck, they will meet in the middle and find us a killer."

"This is insane! I don't cry, let alone get hysterical! When can I get my old self back?" Mac shakes her head and begins pacing. "I'm fed up with being locked away and scared to answer a phone. Maybe Williams can give me some information."

Mac marches herself up the stairs. Her phone sits on the desk, and she stares at it because it makes her nervous. What if something happens to her dad or Spencer while they're protecting her? How could she face her mom? She can't fathom not having him in her life, and she never imagined she would meet someone like him at the agency. But, now that she has, she doesn't want to lose him. She wants to sit and talk like he promised.

A loud noise comes from the first floor, and it rattles Mac. She bolts down the steps two at a time. When Mac reaches the kitchen door and finds Spencer lying on the floor, she races over to him and talks rapidly. "Are you hurt? What's wrong? Can I get you anything? Look at me!" Then she shakes him.

Spencer squints out of one eye and looks up at her. "Why are you yelling at me? I can hear, but I'm out of breath." Spencer sits up, and Mac slides down the wall next to him and lays her head on his shoulder.

"What happened, Spencer? And where is dad?"

"I ran way too far in dress clothes in this heat. Myles is securing the ATV. We saw nothing. He must have realized we knew he was out there. So he left in a hurry. Myles is considering having cameras installed at the entrance to the driveway unless we move."

"Nice. Too bad we didn't think of it two weeks ago." Although no one knew we would be here this long either.

"I agree. Who would have thought the guy would show up here again? He is either bold or stupid. I haven't decided which one yet."

Mac inhales a deep breath trying to gather her wits. "So what's next? Start on the comparisons or call Williams for an update on the middle name?"

Mac calls Williams to follow-up about the James Campbellton she found on the roster. She wants this guy's middle name, but she can't find it on any of her records. Williams is unavailable. The call goes straight to his voice mail. So Mac sits down at the desk and begins sorting her email. She dropped her other FBI cases when she became a target. Mac forwards a few emails to other agents who are picking up her slack. Further down the list, she comes across an email that troubles her. The subject is, *Do you know your partner?* Mac is uncertain at first, but she convinces herself to open the email. She reads it, and then

167

she rereads it. The email asks the same question as to the subject line. It is absolutely the weirdest email she has ever received. Mac leans back in her chair as she ponders the question. She feels like she knows most things about Spencer but not everything. But do you honestly know anyone? Does Mac question Spencer's loyalty to her and the agency? She tells herself she's wasting valuable time going down this line of thought. Spencer has been with her around the clock. There is no way on earth it involved him. Right?

Mac walks down to the lab. Myles and Spencer have their heads together on the comparison. They choose features on the sketch to match the same ones to the pictures of the current FBI agents in Atlanta. Mac stands back and watches Spencer and his mannerisms. She'll have to ask him about the email because she can't just let it go. Still, he just doesn't seem like the type who would betray her. She hopes he feels the same way about her that she does about him. She is counting on Spencer's promise.

Myles turns around first and asks, "Hey there, any news from Williams?"

"Nope. I left a message on his voice mail. What about you?"

Spencer replies, first. "We're just about ready to start on the comparisons. We found several significant areas to pick from on the sketch. With any luck, we'll find a match! Myles hit the start button."

"Done. Now we wait. With three hundred or so agents, it will take about an hour. Let's eat while we wait."

They walk to the kitchen, where Mary puts the finishing touches on sandwich plates.

"Grab a plate and go. Myles, tell David lunch is ready." Mary instructs as she points a spatula at Myles.

Mac and Spencer pick up their plates and head for the TV room. Spencer bites into his sandwich when his phone rings. The caller ID says Williams, so Spencer answers.

"Tell Mac she might be on to something about this, James Campbellton. His middle name is Seth. However, the birthdate is one day off from what we have on his information sheet. So we have Stubin and Lacey headed to his last known address. My other phone is ringing. I'll call back as soon as I hear something." Williams clicks off. Spencer can't believe his ears. They have something! He turns around, and Mac is staring at him because waiting patiently for any update is problematic. He shares the news.

"You are kidding me? We have a solid lead. I can't believe it!" Mac raises her arms above her head in celebration.

"Sorry! I'm just so happy we'll find this guy and put him away! Let's go tell dad!"
Mac grabs Spencer's hand as he places his sandwich plate on the table, and she pulls him toward the door.

Myles walks toward Mac and Spencer when he notices the excitement on Mac's face. "What's going on?"

"Agent Williams called Spencer, and he confirmed James Campbellton's middle name is Seth. Agents Stubin and Lacey are on their way to James Campbellton's last known residence now to check it out. So we're in wait mode again," Mac explains.

Myles asks, "Where does this James guy live? Is it local? Also, get Chastain to run James Campbellton's financials. We need to verify no one is paying him off for the murders."

Spencer looks at Mac, then back at Myles. "We don't know where he lives because Agent Williams didn't give me a chance to ask him. Williams had a call holding for him. I'll contact Chastain."

With his phone to ear, Spencer speaks with Chastain about James Campbellton's financials. He agrees to start on them right away.

"Well. I have work for us in the meantime," Myles adds. "We can go look at the matches the comparisons have hit on so far. Don't forget your lunch."

They scoop up their lunch plates. "Let's go," said Mac. "I need to keep busy, anyway. How many hits are there so far?"

"We have twenty-seven hits on the eyes and the nose. Those are the most predominant features in the sketch. I haven't viewed them yet."

Chapter 15

Mac leads the way to the lab. They take their seats and view the screen where Myles will show the matched comparisons. Once Myles hits the start button, they wait for the show to begin. They made their way through eighteen matches when number nineteen popped open. Mac draws in a sharp breath. She doesn't realize she's holding her breath until Spencer tells her to breathe. Mac turns and gawks at Spencer. Then she looks back at the screen with wide eyes. Drake stares at them with his dark eyes. Mac feels like Drake is staring right through her.

Spencer questions Myles, "Are you kidding me? Drake matches the sketch with his eyes and nose."

Myles taps several buttons on the computer, and lines and dots appear on the screen. These lines and dots highlight the areas that match both pictures. Spencer takes his time with the review, but in the end, he agrees with the computer. They match. Spencer has a hard time believing this.

"Is there a way to put this one picture back in the system and add more areas to compare just to make sure?" Spencer runs his hand through his hair. How can Drake match the sketch?

Myles says, "Yes. What other areas are you thinking?"

"Let's add chin and cheekbones. I need more data if I'm to confront Drake. I need it to be indisputable evidence."

Mac asks, "How long has Drake been with the agency?"

Spencer shrugs his shoulders as he's unsure. "Somewhere around fifteen years, if I remember. He was already with the agency when I started."

Spencer is all consumed on this Drake thing. Has he missed something with Drake? He thought they were friends. They worked out together. Drake never acted like he had many friends, and he always seemed like a loner. Spencer keeps asking himself one question, did I help Drake out by feeding him information on the investigation? Spencer paces the hallway. He tries to work this out, but he's unsure how. Everything makes sense now that he has confirmation with Drake asking questions. Drake being in Knoxville at the same time as one shooting is strange, indeed. Why would Drake do this? There is nothing to gain by murdering other agents unless someone is paying him. He knows he'll spend the rest of his life in prison if he lives through everything.

Myles breaks Spencer's train of thought. "Hey Spencer, can you come here? Got something else for you."

"Swell," mutters Spencer as he heads into the lab.

Myles and Mac stare at the screen. For this picture, not all lines and dots match for this one.
"What exactly am I looking at it?" Spencer asks as he tilts his head from side to side, trying to understand.

Mac explains, "These are the comparisons you asked for using Drake's picture. As you can see, the sketch doesn't entirely match with Drake."

"So. Okay. Several attributes match but not all. That's interesting. Somebody tell me what it means?"

Myles speaks. "Either Abby didn't get the sketch right, or the killer isn't Drake. But I wonder because the matching points are dead on—pardon the pun—the eyes and the nose. They pretty much make up the face. Wouldn't you say?"

"I would say so," adds Mac.

Spencer answers his phone on the second ring. It's Stubin.

"Hey, Spencer. You need to see James Campbellton's apartment. I would send you photos, but it won't do it justice. Come on over before I call the crime lab. Bring Myles if David can watch the house. Someone needs to stay with Mac. The address is in your text messages."

"On my way."

When Spencer ends the call, he shares Stubin's request. Myles and Spencer search for David. They find him pacing through the house, peering out the windows. Myles and Spencer explain the situation, and David agrees to watch Mac and Mary. David understands no one gets close to the windows or doors.

Mac watches this exchange, and she asks, "Any chance I can get a ride with you? I sure would like to see this grand apartment."

Spencer just looks at her as a grin spreads across his face. "No, I want you in one piece when I get back."

Mac watches as Spencer, and her dad gets into another black Suburban and speeds down the driveway.

Spencer glances at his phone when it pings. He waits for the address to appear so Myles can tell him which way to go when they arrive at the main road. "Should I hit I-75 south or Highway 41 south? I'm not sure which one is closest and less busy. The address is in Vinings."

Myles punches in the address on his GPS and says, "Hold on. We need to turn around."
Spencer brakes hard, tires squealing, and he completes a one-eighty turn in the road. Myles grabs the door handle and states, "Let's take the back roads. We can be there in twenty minutes if traffic cooperates."

Spencer's nerves work overtime as his left leg bounces up and down so fast it makes him nauseous. What is in this guy's apartment? Bodies? Please don't let it be any more bodies or body parts. However, we need something to incriminate this jerk and send him away for life.
Twenty minutes later, they pull up outside the apartment. Stubin and Chastain are walking around outside of a four-story frame building. Seth's apartment is on the top left. Lacey is still inside, trying to fathom the scene. Stubin tells Spencer and Myles to brace for a shock.

They enter the apartment, and both are speechless. Every available wall space in sight is covered in photos of the targeted agents. Pictures in the daytime and photographs taken in the nighttime. Photos at work and images at home. The most disturbing is a life-size photo of Mac as the centerpiece. Was Mac the reason for all this killing? She is the prize. But why?

Spencer stands in the middle of the room and turns circles. He can't believe the number of pictures. There is no speck of paint on any walls in the family room, kitchen, or eating area. He contemplates not going into the bedroom for fear of what it holds.

Myles speaks first. "Unbelievable." He shakes his head from side to side, trying to reason this situation.

Spencer enters the room and notices Myles staring at the ceiling. Spencer slowly lifts his head, and there are enormous pictures of Mac plastered to the top. They're like the ones in the family room. She's in the shower, jogging, eating, talking to Williams in the office. Next, she visits the gym and then the grocery store. It continues. Amazed at what he sees, the knot in Spencer's stomach grows to the size of a grapefruit. Myles is dumbfounded as he has witnessed nothing of this nature before. They stare at each other since neither has a response.

Spencer thanks Stubin, and he and Myles head for the car.

"It doesn't appear he's stayed here in a while. There is dust on the furniture and unopened mail on the kitchen counter. What's your opinion?" Spencer questions.

"A sick person lives here, but what concerns me is I don't understand how he got these pictures by himself. Several photos are while she's inside the FBI office. Like the one where Mac is drinking coffee. He had to have had help. That is the scary part."

Spencer receives a text message. He digs for his phone when Myles receives an alert too.

"What now?" he asks. Spencer retrieves his first since Myles is driving. Mac wants to know if Drake has a brother.

Spencer shrugs his shoulders. "I don't know. Do you?"

Myles shakes his head no. Myles smiles. "Mac is wondering if Drake has a brother and if Drake and his brother are doing this together. I raised a smart girl."

"Yes, sir, you did. I'm calling Williams." Spencer couldn't hit the speed dial fast enough.
Williams answers and Spencer asks about Drake and if he has a brother.

"I think he has a half-brother that lives around here somewhere. I don't remember his name, but I seem to recall he came through the academy. Oh my. Don't tell me. No—it can't be. Let me call you back."

The hair on Spencer's neck stands straight out. "Get us home *now*!"

Myles floors it as he blows the horn at the cars traveling in front of them. Spencer explains Williams agrees that Mac has figured out the missing piece. Drake and his half-brother are the so-called masterminds behind this crazy plot. I pray Drake's involvement was unknown to him. "Call Mac. Tell her what transpired and that they need to get somewhere safe. We are ten minutes out. Then call David and tell him."

Spencer and Myles rush home to find all the windows and doors intact and the blinds pulled. They enter the house with guns drawn because they're unsure of what they'll find. They creep through the house and clear each room on their way upstairs. All the doors are closed. "Odd," mutters Myles. They don't close the doors when they're home. After they cleared the second bedroom, Spencer's phone issues another ping, he reads the text message and starts laughing. He stands and points at Myles.

"You can come out now. We're searching the house. You scared us to death having all the doors closed."

Mac, Mary, and David come out of the hallway closet with grins on their faces. They meet in the middle of the hall.

Spencer tells Mac she figured out the puzzle. Drake has a half-brother who lives in the area. He used to live in the apartment where they were this afternoon. He tries to explain what they found without alarming her, but it doesn't work. Mac goes ballistic. She stomps her feet as she walks around, and she runs her fingers through her hair time and again. As an FBI agent, how is it possible that someone followed her and took those pictures without noticing them? Did any of the other agents realize they were being photographed?

Spencer says, "Well, you thought you were being watched, remember? You said so yourself."

"Yeah, I remember. I wish I could have found Seth and finished him then."

Myles brings the group back to reality. "We have to get these guys alive. I'm afraid when they find out we know their identity, everything will change. They might start shooting at any officers, not just the FBI. Has Williams called back yet?"

"No," replies Spencer. "And neither has Stubin. He was staying at the apartment to wait on the crime scene techs. The apartment should make for interesting grid work. The recovered evidence should be something to see!"

Mac speaks. "I want to go to headquarters and confront Drake. I want an answer about why all this started. What provoked them to go to this much trouble to kill FBI agents? And why me? What did I do to warrant being a target?"

Mac turns around, and both Myles and Spencer shake their heads no. Then, she smiles at them and says, "You both look like bobbleheads. I said I wanted to go to the office, but I can't, not until we capture this guy. Has anyone asked for a picture of James Campbellton from the FBI academy yet? I would like to see how close the sketch is to what Abby described."

"Let's go to the lab. We'll search the database for the photo. Williams had the FBI lab send the info to me," replies Myles. He continues, "I'm proud of you, Mac because you connected the dots. You were always the one to get the solution first. Your brothers were always mad at you for figuring out the problems first! Excellent job, kiddo!"

"Thanks, dad. I knew it was something simple. It was always on the tip of my tongue."

Spencer says in a soft tone, "I never knew Drake had a half-brother. He shared nothing about his family. I asked him too. I don't even know if his parents are still living."

"Don't take it personally. It's not your fault he started killing. We just have to find him. That's the crucial thing," Mac states.

Mac's cell phone rings. She stands and stares at it because she doesn't know if she should answer. Spencer walks over to the desk and lifts it. He glances at the ID. Then, he hands the phone to Mac. Mac has a puzzled expression on her face, but she takes the phone and notices Agent Williams calling.

She quickly answers it. "Hi, Agent Williams."

"Hi yourself, Mac. How are you today? No, wait, don't answer me. Let me share what I have learned in the last bit of time. You were right. Drake has a half-brother: James Seth Campbellton. The FBI ousted him from the academy. I'm having his file pulled. Also, Stubin called, and the crime scene techs located a laptop hidden under the mattress. They will report whatever information they find, which I hope is a bunch of incriminating evidence as the pictures aren't enough. Also, I haven't seen Drake around the office today, so he might be unaware we're onto him. I have told no one but you, Spencer, and Myles. I don't want him slipping through the cracks and disappearing on us."

"Me either. I want to confront Drake when this is over, and he's behind bars because I want to know why me. I did nothing to him, let alone his half-brother, whom I knew nothing about. Is Honeycutt still in custody? If so, someone needs to visit him and find out how he met James Seth. They were not in the same class at the academy. Not sure it will help the case, but I would like the information just for my curiosity."

"When Stubin returns from the crime scene, I'll ask him and Baxter to speak with Honeycutt since they have already met each other. Stubin seems to think Honeycutt is holding more information than he's sharing, anyway. Chastain had an incorrect birth date for James, so he has requested financials again. I'll check in later. Good job, Mac. Just sorry, your first big case had to be your own!"

Williams disconnects the call, and Mac stares at her phone with a grin on her face.

Mac and Spencer are alone in the office while the others pretend to be working. Spencer wants to hold her, touch her, kiss her, but she's still just out of reach. He can't risk anything yet. So they sit there and stare into each other eyes, and she reaches out and touches his hand. The sparks run from the tip of her toes to the top of her head. She watches as Spencer's eyes grow dark. Mac's face flushes. She's never felt this way before about a man. She isn't sure how to handle it. But she'll try. Spencer is still holding her hand when he asks her to stand. So they stand in the middle of the office, just holding each other, not knowing what tomorrow will bring.

Myles calls for Mac and Spencer. They share a grin as they head for the lab. When they enter, Myles stares at a picture on the gigantic screen. Mac glimpses the image, and her breath catches in her throat.

"Wow. Is that Drake? Or Seth?" asks Mac.

Myles answers, "Seth."

Mac's eyes are playing games. Drake and Seth could pass for brothers and no half to it. They both got dark hair and eyes.

"That is amazing. Whichever parent they share, they must have had dark hair and eyes. Abby's sketch nailed it. It's definitely Seth," Mac says as she speaks to Spencer.

Spencer has a strange look on his face, and Mac senses he is concentrating. He's in deep thought.

Mac walks over to him and touches him on his arm to bring him out of his zone.

He gives his head a gentle shake and says, "I want to be the one to question Drake, and I want to be the one to arrest Seth. The brotherly relation means nothing to me. I'm ready to end this melee."

Spencer's speech astonishes Mac, but she agrees with it. She's ready to end this nonsense too.

Myles suggests they email Williams and include this picture of Seth. The picture should confirm everything they shared with him tonight. Myles says his good nights, and he goes off to the bed as exhaustion takes hold. It is easier working cases on unfamiliar people than on your daughter, especially when your daughter is a target for murder.

Mac and Spencer walk to their bedrooms and say their good nights. Both are in deep thought when they separate. Would tomorrow be the day they find Seth?

Mac wakes up to Spencer knocking on her door. She jumps up and runs to it. She opens it and realizes she is staring at Spencer. His mouth hangs open as he glimpses Mac.

Mac says, "What's wrong?"

Spencer stammers, and he spits out, "Oh, sorry. You are gorgeous. Are you this pretty every morning?"

Mac tries to play it off by smoothing down her hair. She looks down and is a little embarrassed to see she only has on a long T-shirt. She hadn't taken the time last night to put on her pajama bottoms before she climbed into bed.

The door closes in Spencer's face as Mac yells through the door, "I'll be out in a minute. Let me get dressed. Whatever you have to say better, be important!"

Spencer leans up against the door frame and chuckles to himself. Oh yeah, he knows he has to have this one. He'll do anything to keep her safe because he wants her like no other person. No one has touched him like Mac. Marriage was not something he regularly pondered about because, with his FBI status, he figured he would be alone forever. He never imagined finding anyone he wanted to live day in and day out with. But now he knows he has.

Spencer has been leaning against the door for two minutes when it opens ever so slightly. Mac steals a quick glimpse to see if Spencer is still there. She had to work up enough nerve to face him, and she's ready for the jokes.

"Come on out. I won't laugh," says Spencer.

"Great! Now I have to listen to your jokes all day. You woke me up from a deep sleep, and I didn't think about my attire. I apologize."

"Don't apologize for my sake. I thoroughly enjoyed it. I could look at you every day." Spencer takes Mac by the upper arm and turns her toward him. He plants a kiss on her that absolutely makes her tingle all over. Mac's eyes grow wide, and then she gives in as her arms close around Spencer's neck. Spencer's embrace brings Mac closer, and she is speechless. They break apart and spend several seconds gazing into each other's eyes. They both realize they are smitten with the other. But they are in the wrong place at the wrong time. Mac is in a life or death situation, and Spencer commits to ending this unthinkable situation.

Mac somehow finds her voice. "So what is so urgent you had to wake me up at 0600."

"We have news. I spoke to Williams at 0530. The CSI team did not find any fingerprints at Seth's, which they expected. The real news is his laptop confirms Drake was a part of this entire thing. Drake was emailing Seth information about the shootings and what was happening with the graduates. Now, we're not sure if Drake was doing this just because he spoke to his brother daily or if he intended to help Seth with his murderous plan. That is still unknown."

"So is it enough information to detain Drake? Or at least question him?"

Spencer continues, "We're still unsure. The lab is still putting the pieces together on the laptop. They are making a timeline of the emails to and from Drake."

"Why would Seth come after me like this? I've never met him before. I have only spoken to Drake a few times."

"Drake wanted to date you, but he felt you were out of his league. Apparently, he shared his desires with his half-brother, and Seth took it from there." Spencer explains.

"Where is Seth now?" Curious, Mac asks.

Spencer didn't want to tell her this, but he relented and told her no one had Seth's location. He hasn't returned to his apartment, and an officer still watches it.

Mac asks, "Where is Drake? I'd like to speak with him."

Spencer lifts his eyebrow. "You're not talking to him until I get a chance at him. There is no way you're leaving this house unless I can talk you into going to the safe house in North Georgia."

"Spencer, you're a genius! That's exactly what we need. We set up the sting at the safe house. Don't talk with Drake yet. Let's use him."

"Mac, this sure is gutsy and borderline reckless. I don't like you being used in that way. Dangerous things happen on stings."

"I know it's a possibility, but what better way to get him to come out? You call Drake and just check in with him. Tell him you're moving me to a safe house and that you need his help, and so on. Play it up big. He needs to assume we know nothing of his half-brother. Drake will get the info to Seth, and then we get our man on our way to the safe house. It will work. Let's run it by Dad. Then we can talk with Williams."

Spencer nods his head in agreement, and they head downstairs for breakfast.
Mary still wears her apron since cooking her guests a vast breakfast. Mac enters the kitchen because she continues her search for her dad.

"Mom, where's dad? I have something to run by him."

"Dear, Myles had an early meeting in Atlanta. He'll return around eleven. David is here if you need him."

Mac glances at Spencer, and he shrugs his shoulders. "We can wait. We need to see if we can
find the connection between Honeycutt and Seth. I still can't find it."

"We'll eat and then head up to the lab. Mom, can you send dad up to the lab when he gets back?"

"Sure will," says Mary as she cleans after breakfast.

Mac sips coffee while she stares at the computer screen. Finally, she asks herself a question. "How old are Honeycutt and Seth?"

"Good question, Mac. Let's search. We should be able to find that information."

"I thought I was alone. I didn't hear you come in."

"You were deep in thought," says Spencer. He types on the keyboard, trying to find the correlation between Honeycutt and Seth. They are familiar with each other. Otherwise, all this killing would be a weird coincidence.

Spencer shakes his head and says, "I don't believe in coincidences."

Mac turns her chair toward Spencer and asks, "What? Were you talking to me?"

Spencer chuckles and answers Mac. "No, I was talking to myself. Just confirming, I don't believe in coincidences. Here we go."

Mac rolls her chair over in front of Spencer's computer to look at his search results. Mac grins from ear to ear. She hit the nail on the head. So this proves Seth and Honeycutt went to high school together. At least they confirmed the killers knew each other.

"Spencer, did Stubin call? I was wondering if they had gotten back to Honeycutt yet."

"Nothing from him yet. Let's call." Spencer digs his cell out of his pocket and dials Stubin.

"Great. Straight to voice mail."

"This will give us time to put our plan down on paper. That way, I can use it to sell dad on the idea of setting up a sting for Seth. Then, once we get Seth, you get to have some alone time with Drake." Mac offered.

"I want to spend time with Drake but not so much about the plan. I'm still a little skeptical because it sounds awful dangerous for you."

Mac listens as a conversation transpires downstairs, and she assumes it is her dad. She tells Spencer she is going downstairs to check. She walks downstairs toward the kitchen only to realize George and David are talking. They're anxious about something. Energy is high. She waits for a second, hoping to gather info as to what they are doing. Unable to make out what they were saying, she descends the stairs slowly. She peers around the corner, hoping her dad is with them. Nope. Just the two guys huddled close to together and talking in quick whispers. When they spot her, they both straighten.

George said, "Mac, get away from the windows. We might have a problem. We were just discussing it. Where is Spencer?"

Mac drops to the floor behind the kitchen island as George waves his arm downward. "Spencer is in the office. We figured out Honeycutt and Seth attended high school together. I was searching for dad when I found you two huddled."

George immediately calls for Spencer. David walks from window to window, checking all the locks and drawing the blinds. Spencer reaches the kitchen in thirty seconds.

"What's up, guys?" Spencer asks as he enters the kitchen. Then he continues, "Mac, why are you on the floor?"

George explains, "The backyard cameras caught movement. We're not sure what kind of movement. It might be an animal or a person. But we felt like we needed to prepare ourselves, just in case."

"I agree," answers Spencer. "Let's rewind the video and see if we can make it out."

"We already tried. But be my guest. Maybe you will spot something we didn't," says David.

They head for the control room, where the surveillance equipment sits. They are waiting to view the video when a loud pop sounds from the kitchen, then crashing glass. Everyone looks at each other, and then they bolt down the stairs with weapons drawn.

Chapter 16

Everyone enters the kitchen at once and stops short when they find the damage. Glass litters the floor from the window's explosion. Mac finds a brick with an envelope attached under the kitchen table. The envelope has Mac's name on it. With a tissue, Mac opens the envelope revealing a slip of paper and a simple message. 'Time is up! 72 hours. Count them down one by one.'

Mac sits down at the kitchen table and stares at the warning. "What kind of sick person does this to another human?"

Spencer interrogates George. "Why didn't the alarms sound? Seth penetrated the backyard because he had to be within throwing distance to get the brick through the window. How did he know we were upstairs?"

George has no answer. He's at a complete loss like the rest of the group.

Mac barks instructions. "Find Mom. I don't want her to get caught up in this. She needs to stay in the middle of the house. And give me a broom. I need to clean this mess. Somebody, please find plywood and cover this window."

Spencer looks at George and David. "She means business. Let's check on the security wires in the backyard. We need to find out how he got into the yard without triggering alarms. Then we'll find a piece of wood for the window."

Myles arrives home to find Spencer and David nailing wood into the window frame. The damage shocks him. "What did I miss? Obviously, it was something big."

Mac explains about the brick and the note. Myles' face turns dark red as he throws out questions to the guys. "Did the intrusion activate the backyard alarm? Have we checked the yard to see why it didn't? Has anybody done anything with the letter yet?"

"Hold on, dad. I told them to fix the window first. It scares Mom to come downstairs now." Mac answers while trying to deescalate the situation.

"I got a little carried away. It frustrates me because I can't explain the security system. I'll check on it myself because I've never had a system so easily penetrated."

Spencer speaks up and says, "Let me save you time. George and I found the cut wires. I have it marked for you. This guy is talented, and he must have training in security systems."

Mac is ready to share her plan with Myles. Everyone is in the kitchen except her mom, which is a good thing. "Dad, I want to talk with you about a plan we developed over the last several hours. This might work to capture Seth. Can you sit with us at the table?"

Myles tries to skip this conversation with excuses, but Mac convinces him to sit with them when she shows him the note and the brick.

Mac explains the plan, and Myles says he needs time. He isn't at all excited about using his only daughter as bait for a madman, although he agrees Seth would come out in the open if he thought he could get his hands on Mac.

"Can you give me until morning to dwell on this plan? I want to work it out in my head and make sure we have forgotten nothing. Is Williams aware of the plan yet?"

Mac shakes her head no. "We haven't shared it. But, dad, if you agree, we need to put the plan into motion tomorrow because twenty-four hours have already passed!"

Mac couldn't sleep—again. She reviews the plan over and over in her head, hoping she has overlooked nothing. Then her mind travels to Spencer. How she loves to look at him and how she enjoys talking and spending time with him. Who would have thought her soul mate was an FBI agent? Tossing and turning, she reads her bedside clock. It was only 0100.—another long night. Wait. What was that noise? Her doorknob turns, the door opens, and she immediately recognizes the silhouette in the doorway. Her breath catches in her throat. Spencer whispers,

"Are you awake?"

"Yes. I can't sleep. Just can't turn the brain off tonight."

Spencer walks over to the bed, and Mac pats the space beside her. "Are you sure you want me in your bed?"

Mac pauses before she replies, "I have never been so sure of anything in my life."

Spencer slides in beside her, and immediately they snuggle. The contact between the two eases the tension of the day. Mac relaxes because she knows Spencer is the man for her.

Both turn groggy with sleep, and they doze off in each other's arms. Spencer wakes with a start. Unsure of the time, he peers over Mac to read the bedside clock. Its red numbers glow 0530, so he slips out of Mac's bed to make his way back to his room.

The kitchen is empty. She expected everyone to be up and at it this morning. Mac just knows today is the day she'll start living again. Twelve days is a long time to spend locked n her parents' house, trying to stay alive. So where is everyone? How come no one is awake yet? Mac pours herself a cup of coffee and takes two sips.

"This isn't right. Someone should be up by this hour," Mac mutters to herself. She places her cup on the counter and looks around. She first walks into the family room, and it's empty. Next, she goes upstairs. The doors are closed—not a pleasant sign. She pulls her weapon and quietly creeps to the office door. She places her ear on the door. Nothing. No one is speaking. Is anyone here? She wants to scream. Mac makes her way to the lab when Spencer opens the door with such force it knocks the breath out of her. They stare at each other, and Mac is so shaken that her knees buckle. Spencer watches the shift in Mac's face and runs to catch her before she hits the ground.

"What are you doing with your service weapon pointed at me?"

"It wasn't pointed at you. No one was around, and I panicked. What are you doing up here, and why wasn't I invited?"

Myles steps forward and begins with an explanation. "We're here for you. We wanted to go over the plan once more. You were sleeping so well that we didn't want to wake you."

Mac straightens herself up as she gives Spencer a sideways glance and holsters her weapon. She hopes no one can read her eyes. Only she and Spencer share their secret. "Well, making noise would have helped. I couldn't find anyone in the house, and I got a little jumpy."

Everyone chuckles at Mac's expense. They head toward the kitchen for breakfast. Afterward, David, George, Spencer, Myles, and Mac sit at the kitchen table. Myles has the plan laid out in front of them. Overall, the plan is simple. They're moving Mac to a safe house in North Georgia. They'll use a decoy vehicle. The kicker is they are calling in Drake for help with the hopes of Drake telling his brother, Seth, their plans. Myles tells Spencer to make the call. Spencer stands from the table and dials Drake. He shares the plan with Drake about moving Mac to the safe house. Spencer asks for Drake's help to drive the decoy vehicle. Drake jumps on the chance to help. The plan takes shape. Now they will wait until 1300.

Spencer phones Agent Williams, advising him of the plan. Astonished, Williams can't believe it involves one of his own. Drake has been part of his team since he walked through the door at FBI headquarters. He can't wrap his head around that one. Drake was always there whenever Williams called on him to handle something. But now that Williams is mulling over this newest tidbit of info, he realizes Drake never spoke of his family. He doesn't remember what became of Seth after they let him go from the FBI academy. Drake and Seth must have talked, and Seth took it upon himself to carry out these murders. It's weird how you can work with someone day in and day out in dangerous situations and never know about their family. Williams puts on his game face and heads out the door to see how things are going when Drake shows up in the doorway of his office.

"Williams, I wanted to reach out to you before I head out. I'm sure you've spoken with Spencer about moving Mac to a safe house."

Williams concedes he has indeed spoken with Spencer. "I'm on pins and needles waiting for today to be over with. I just want Mac safe. Hopefully, the transfer to the safe house will go without incident."

Drake nods his head yes and turns around. He exits the building without speaking to anyone.
Williams stands in the doorway, staring at the back of Drake's head, and waits several seconds until Drake exits the outer door of the office. He then calls Spencer and advises that Drake is on his way, and he's acting strange. Spencer replies with a chuckle. "Is there any other way for Drake to act?"

"No, I guess not," Williams answered, sounding defeated.

Mac is anxious. Why did they decide on 1300? They should have set it up for earlier in the day. She glances at Spencer, but he continues to pour over the same maps. He hasn't left those maps today. His face shows determination. With Spencer's eyebrows bunched together, slight wrinkles form around his eyes. Here I go again, thinks Mac, starting with the eyes. Those eyes are unbelievable. If you look close enough, Spencer's emotions are all written in them. But she has too much to concentrate on today. Get through this mess, and then she and Spencer could have the talk they waited for. She pivots her attention away from Spencer.
He notices a subtle change in her attitude. "What's wrong? Are you mad at me?"

Mac chuckles. "Heaven's no. Just too much thinking on my part. I'm ready for this to be over."

"Right. Drake should be here any minute. David, George, and your dad are in their respective spots. The plan is ready."

About that time, a knock came from the front door.

Mac whispers to Spencer, "Showtime!" Then she trots over to answer the door.

Drake stands on the front porch like a schoolboy picking his girl up on their first date. Mac steps aside to allow Drake to enter the house. Chills run up her spine as she lets this guy into her parents' home. She peers at Spencer, and Spencer sees the angst in her eyes. Mac wants to wrestle Drake to the ground and ask why he's doing this to her. Why would he help murder fellow agents? Instead, she follows Drake into the kitchen, and they sit at the table with Spencer as he goes over the plan, including the route they will take to the safe house. Spencer and Mac watch Drake's every move. Each time his mouth twitches, Mac looks over at Spencer. By the time they finish with Drake, Mac's stomach is in knots. She asks them to give her a few moments upstairs with her mom. She heads upstairs, knowing Spencer will talk to Drake. He has questions before they go through with this plan.

Spencer glances over at Drake, trying not to show his emotions, and asks, "Anything going on at the office today?"

"No, not that I am aware." Drake is always a man of few words.

Spencer adds, "When this investigation is over, we can get back to the meeting in the gym. I need a good workout."

Drake's eyes scan back and forth across the kitchen. Then, finally, he gives in and says, "I'd like that."
Spencer notices Drake is on pins and needles. He can't be still. He keeps walking past the window as if he is waiting on something.

"Anything out there?"

"Uh, no. Just looking around. This house is a beauty." Drake states as he takes in the surroundings.

Mac walks into the kitchen and instantly feels the tension. She's ready to get the show on the road. "It's two minutes until one. Can we leave yet?" Mac directs her question at Spencer.

He backs away from the maps. "Yes—load up. Drake, you have your assignment. Good luck, and we'll see you soon."

Drake answers with a nod of his head and then walks to the door.

Spencer walks Mac to the Suburban. He looks into her eyes and sees just what he needs to see. He wants to hug her and take her back inside to safety. "Get in and buckle your seatbelt," Spencer says with a grin.

She obliges without a word.

Drake drives the decoy vehicle, and Spencer follows. Their route will have them travel north on I-75 for a while. Then they'll cut over on Highway 140 to go to the northwest corner of Georgia. They suspect Seth will try to ambush them on the road, somewhere in Walker County. Agent Williams notified the Walker County sheriff of the impending attack. They will have necessary medical personnel on standby. No one knows how Seth will attempt to get to Mac. He didn't have enough time to stake out a location like the other kills. So he might just shoot them as they drive down the road.

Spencer steals a glance at Mac, as she stares out her window. She watches the road as it flies past.

"A penny for your thoughts?" Spencer asked.

A grin spreads across her face, but she can't face him. "Nope—not right now. You don't want to know what I am thinking."

"You'll be safe. I don't want you considering this guy will take you from me."

"I can't wait for this to be behind me, behind us. But we have a lot to get through today, so I'm trying to concentrate on it."

"I understand. I'll leave you with your thoughts. We have thirty minutes or so before we hit the back roads. That's when things can turn dicey."

Spencer exits the interstate onto SR 140 without incident. This highway runs east and west, and they turn west. Mac searches for anything out of the ordinary. Drake remains in the lead. No patrol cars around. No cars stopped on the side of the road. The road is four lanes through town. Then it drops to a two-lane highway. It's a pleasant ride with trees on each side. But then, Mac thinks I'm in an unfamiliar area if something happens. How could I lead the police to us? But she says nothing.

Spencer looks over at her. "We're heading west on SR 140. It will intersect with SR 27. At the intersection, we go north. I just thought you might like information on your location."

"Thanks," Mac answers sheepishly. She's never been with someone who had the uncanny ability to read her mind. They drive for another hour. The terrain is all the same: two-lane roads and lots of pastures and trees. Mac sucks in a breath when she realizes they're traveling up a mountain.

"Are we going up there?" Mac points to Pigeon Mountain.

"Yes, we are. The roads are curvy, with steep drop-offs. If you get car sick, look straight ahead, and you should be okay."

"Why did you pick a house way up here?" Mac questions as she studies the terrain.

"The answer is obvious. Don't you agree?"

"Yes, I guess you're right. How much further?"

"We'll be there in under forty-five minutes." Spencer picks up his cell phone and punches a number. His phone chirps twice, and he reports, "We're ready."

Mac gets a weird sensation in the pit of her stomach. It wouldn't go away. She tries to conjure happier times, but she has had an unsettled feeling that things will not go her way today. "Thank you," she quietly says to Spencer.

"You don't have to thank me. But I accept your gratitude. Why are you so down in the dumps suddenly? It will work out."

"I just have a strange feeling something bad will happen. I won't be able to make it if I lose one of you. All of you have spent so much time protecting me. I couldn't handle it." Mac states with a quivering voice.

"First off, nothing will happen. Other than us getting this guy off of the streets. Second, I want to be with you. I honestly didn't want to let you out of my sight. After this, we will have that talk we discussed."

"I would like that." Then she turns her head toward the window. She doesn't want Spencer to see the unshed tears in her eyes.

The safe house is fifteen minutes away. Drake slows his speed. Spencer rises on the wheel of the truck while Mac sits on the floorboard. She is worried to death about the shooter aiming at him.
They are yelling at each other so loud neither one recognizes the sound of a ringing cell phone.

"Wait. Stop yelling. My cell phone is vibrating. I missed the call. It's Drake."

"What, Drake?"

"I can't remember the name of the road I need to turn onto. Isn't it close?" Drake asked.

"Yes. Two roads to the left."

They disconnect, and Mac sighs. She's ready. She raises herself from the floorboard and pushes herself into the seat as they turn into the driveway of the safe house. Mac surveys the area by taking in the charming one-story home on a slab. The home has a two-car attached garage and a flat backyard. Spencer exits first and checks around the house's perimeter. He finds nothing, including no tracks of any kind. Maybe they are safe, and Seth has stopped this nonsense. Spencer walks around to the passenger door and opens it for Mac. She steps out, wanting to run as they stand at the end of the driveway.

"Can I take a peek inside?"

"Sure. No problem." Spencer hands her the key to the front door.

Mac's eyes follow the driveway toward the front door. As she passes between Spencer and Drake, the report of a gunshot echo in the mountains. Spencer dives for Mac while Drake drops to his knees. Spencer grunts when he lands on top of Mac. His grunt scares Mac. She struggles to lift his shoulder because when they landed on the ground, it pinned one of her arms behind her. She maneuvers enough to lift Spencer from her body so she can see his face. When she pulls her hand back, blood covers it.

"Spencer is shot. Drake, help me!"

Drake doesn't answer. When Mac pushes Spencer off of her, she pats his pockets, searching for his cell phone. As she stands on shaky knees, she realizes she's alone. Another shot flies past her head and ends up in the front window of the house. Mac hears footsteps on loose gravel, but she can't discern their location. She runs to the truck, jumping in to find Spencer's phone still in the console. She pushes the speed dial button he showed her earlier for the Walker County Sheriff, and he answers.

"My name is Mac Morris, and someone shot my partner. His breathing is shallow. Send someone now." She disconnects after giving her location, and then she tries her dad. No answer. She sends him a text. He responds by sending a letter, K.

Mac sees a man dressed in black running toward a black sedan parked alongside the road two hundred yards away. With her service weapon in position, she runs toward him, yelling at him to stop. The man in the ski mask stops, drops to one knee, places a rifle to his shoulder, and fires one round. Mac recognizes the stance and falls to the ground just in time to miss the bullet.

Well, almost. The bullet grazes the top of her left shoulder. She glances down, and blood cascades down the front of her shirt and into her vest. When she looks up, she hears the guy driving away at a top rate of speed. She calls her dad again and tells him about the wounds both she and Spencer suffered.

"I heard the gunshots, but I couldn't get to you fast enough. David is south of our location, waiting for the car to pass him. He'll stop him. George is coming to pick me up. So, stay with Spencer and go to the hospital with him. You'll be safe there. Any sign of Drake?"

"No, the first shot sent him running. Dad, be careful."

The ambulance, deputies, and EMTs arrive at the house. Spencer is now conscious and standing on his own, although he's a little shaky. He swatches Mac as she walks back to the house.

"Where did you go? Why are you bleeding?"

"It's just a flesh wound. I'll tell you all about it when we get you to the hospital. Guys, load him into the ambulance, and I'll follow." The EMTs hand Mac gauze pads to staunch her blood. She passes Spencer's cell phone to him through the EMT.

Chapter 17

The ambulance drives away from the house, and Mac wonders if David stopped the guy from leaving the mountain. A half-mile later, the ambulance comes upon a black Suburban stopped on the edge of the street. Mac calls Spencer to advise him she is stopping to check on David, and she watches as the ambulance drives away.

"David, what happened? Where is the guy with the ski mask?" David points. "Down there about a thousand feet. I don't see how anyone could survive that fall. But we need to make sure he is still with the vehicle."

Just then, Myles and George show up at the scene along with the sheriff.

"Sheriff, is there a way to get to the car down there?"

"Yes, we can go to the bottom of the mountain and take the fire road. We'll get close to it, and then we'll have to walk in the rest of the way."

Myles smiles. "Lead the way."

Mac climbs back into her SUV to continue the trip to the ER while Myles, George, and David follow the Sheriff. Spencer is in the emergency room, getting stitches, and Mac sits in the room next to his getting her wound dressed, when Drake walks into Mac's room. Mac does a double-take.

"Nice of you to make an appearance. Where did you come from? You left me alone after the first shot." Mac stated with a furrowed brow and a tilted head.

"Yeah—I thought I saw a scope circle through the trees, so I tried to locate it. I heard all the commotion, but the mountain roads confused me. It took me a while to figure out where I was. I came here as soon as possible. Are you okay? And where is Spencer?"

Mac stares at him because she's unsure if she can trust this guy. "He is next door, getting stitches in his shoulder."

A split second later, Drake walks out of her room and steps next door. Mac grimaces when Spencer yells at Drake so loud the entire ER hears the conversation.

"What is wrong with you? How could you come back here after this? Why didn't you tell us you had a half-brother that resembles you?"

Drake doesn't bat an eye. He stares directly at Spencer, waiting for the barrage of words to stop. Drake tells Spencer the same excuse he gave Mac. Spencer doesn't buy it. Finally, Drake realizes what Spencer is saying.
"You think I'm involved with these killings? Is that it? You used me to get to my half-brother. How could you use me? Tell me, no!" Drake turns away from Spencer while rubbing his hands down his face.

"Yes, we did. We have proof you've been sharing information with Seth. He has been using this information to kill newly graduated agents."

"You're kidding me, right? Seth has been fine since the FBI let him go. Granted, being an FBI agent was all we talked about when we were little, but I thought he was okay as a cop. After all, Seth's dad was a cop who was killed in the driveway of their family home. He was in uniform and heading to work the day shift. Seth said he enjoyed his job as a police officer, but he mentioned he would have liked his dad to see him." Drake leaned over, placing his hands on his knees like he was trying to stop himself from passing out.

Mac listens to the conversation from the doorway. "Why does Seth have a different last name? Do you have different dads?"

"Same, mom. Different dads. Both of our dads left us at an early age. Like I told Spencer, Seth's dad died in the line of duty, and mine just left. Mom raised us until one day, she just didn't come back either. So I raised Seth until I left for the army."

Drake shakes his head in disbelief. "This mess is unbelievable. Was Seth in the car that careened over the mountain?"

Mac defers to Spencer for an answer. "It's a possibility," Spencer grumbles.

Drake looks around the ER and then bolts out the door. Mac chases him, but she misses him. Mac walks back into the room with Spencer.

"Did we misjudge Drake?"

"No. There was something in Drake's reaction to my comments. His eyes glazed over, and his mouth started twitching." Spencer explained.

"It could be he didn't want to believe Seth is capable of something like this."

As Spencer shook his head he offered. "I don't know, but as soon as this guy finishes with my stitches, we're going back to the scene. Have you checked in with Agent Williams?"

Mac nods her head yes and then adds, "The CSI team is at the house now. They found the slug. Williams said I could do the ballistics work on it. They also found shoe prints and will match those with the ones they found at Seth's apartment. If the guy had not parked so far in the woods, we would have him by now."

Spencer looks down at the tech as she puts the finishing touches on his stitches. Mac chuckles as she turns her head. "Shut up," he says as he tries to jump off of the gurney. Mac reaches over and grabs his arm.

"Hold on, Spencer. You're shaky and with a green pallor. Maybe you should hang out here for a little while."

"Not a chance. Go get the car while they finish my paperwork." Mac obeys and leaves Spencer sitting in a wheelchair by the emergency room exit holding a clipboard.

Mac's cell phone rings when she's halfway to the car. She grabs it before looking at the caller ID. She chastises herself for not checking first as she hesitantly answers.

"Hi, Mac. We are at the foot of the mountain where the car landed. No sign of the driver. Can you believe someone takes a spill like this and walks away? There is evidence of injury. We have several locals that are tracking the driver for us. It appears the driver headed back toward town. What is your status, and how is Spencer?"

"Hey, dad. Spencer is waiting for me to take him back to the scene. They stitched him, and his arm is in a sling. He won't be using it for a few days. But he should be fine. I'll call you when we get closer."

Spencer climbs into the passenger side of the vehicle. Mac buckles his seat belt for him. Once situated, Mac advises Spencer of her dad's call. It amazes Spencer that the driver walked away from the accident too. That is absolutely unbelievable! Spencer digs his cell phone out of his pocket and calls Myles. Did Drake return to the scene? Myles says he hasn't seen Drake at all. And then he asks George and David. Neither of them has seen Drake either. When Spencer finishes his call with Myles, he turns quiet and goes into his own world. He tries to put the pieces together.

She lets him simmer a while. Then she asks, "Walk me through what we have so far."

Spencer pauses for several seconds. Then, he reviews the details from the first murder to the last, from Honeycutt to Seth and then from Seth to Drake.

Mac adds, "We can't put Drake at any of the murders, right?"

"Well, we didn't look. Drake didn't tie himself to things until the end. We need to check his travels and see if he was near any other murders."

"He was in Tennessee, remember? Williams asked him to take photos for us."

"Oh, yeah. I forgot about that. Wonder if the captain would mind talking with us? I would like to hear how Drake acted when he was there."

"That's an excellent idea," replies Mac. Mac has something nipping at her mind, but she can't pull it out. There is something she's missing, but it stays right out of touch.

Mac and Spencer are almost back to the scene when Williams calls Spencer. A man reported a stolen truck from a farm not too far from their location. Spencer tells Williams they'll check it out. Mac takes a left on a curvy two-lane road. The road is narrow, with double yellow lines down the middle and woods on both sides. She travels as fast as possible when they come upon a vast expanse of beautiful land. Mountains in the background and small farmhouses dot the area. The farmer stands at the end of his driveway, waiting on the pair. They both exit the vehicle. Mac has a bandaged shoulder with blood-stained clothes, and Spencer's arm is in a sling with the sleeve of his shirt cut off. The farmer doesn't know what to say. He just stares at them. Mac explains the earlier incident. The farmer asks them if they need to sit. Mac smiles and takes the farmer by his elbow and guides him back to the house. They end up on the screen porch.

Spencer is eager for information. So he asked the farmer, "can you tell us what happened?"

The farmer replies, "Yeah, sure. I didn't know you would be in such a big hurry. I went out to the barn to get my truck to run to town for the missus. The barn's lock hung open from the loop where someone cut it, and they stole my truck. I found a lot of blood. Whoever took the truck won't get too far bleeding like that."

Spencer stands and asks, "Can you show us?"

"Sure can." The farmer takes them out of the back door. They walk to the barn. Some barn this turns out to be.

207

Spencer has never seen a barn like this. Three cars and two tractors in this structure. Concrete floors, fluorescent lights, two bathrooms, and a TV room.

Spencer glances over at Mac. "My kind of barn."

The farmer shows them the pool of blood on the outside of the barn door, but there was nothing on the inside. There are no signs the suspect used the facilities either. To preserve the blood spot, Spencer asks the farmer for a bucket. They also instruct the farmer not to touch the blood because a CSI team is coming over to take samples and pictures.

Once they finish scouting the area, Mac asks the farmer, "Can you give us the truck's description and the tag number? We need to get a BOLO out for it."

The farmer describes it as an older Chevrolet Silverado. Had it so long, he can't remember the year: blue and silver. The tag number is AGT 9933. Spencer and Mac move toward their vehicle.

"Are you hungry? We have good eats up here."

Mac and Spencer bow out of eating with the farmer. Instead, they drive back down the same road toward the main highway.

"Now our guy has a new set of wheels. If he is bleeding as bad as they say, he can't go too far in that condition without medical help. He should be weak and tired. Is it possible he drove back into town for help?"

Spencer gathers his thoughts for a minute. "He would wait on his brother somewhere. Seth expects Drake to be here because Drake told him. I just don't know where they would meet. Let's go back toward town. I am getting hungry anyway."

Mac drives around a little while, passing a twenty-four-hour breakfast joint with a ton of customers. They can tell because the parking lot is almost full. Mac notices a vehicle backed in toward the back of the restaurant. But it doesn't register as special to her, and they continue. They find another fast-food place and enter. Sitting at the table with their mouths stuffed with chicken sandwiches, it hits Mac.

"Oh my gosh. Hurry, Spencer. I know Seth's location."

"What are you talking about? How do you know where he is?"

"I saw a truck backed in at that breakfast place, but it didn't click until now. Drake's favorite food group is breakfast."

Spencer glares back at her. "And who told you this?"

Mac senses petty jealousy creeping out of Spencer, and she likes it. "He told Stubin that tidbit of information one day at our task force meeting."

"Well, well. A brief history of Drake. I've worked with him in the gym for years and never knew of this. Grab your drink. Let's go!"

They run to the vehicle. Mac fastens Spencer's seat belt and then her own. She doesn't want to attract any attention, so they drive by at the standard speed limit. Mac sighs when she realizes the truck is still there. Only this time, she makes out a silhouette. Someone is in the driver's seat.

"Do you think he knows we are after him?" Mac asks Spencer.

"Yes. He has a good idea. We've driven past two times, and both of us are staring at his truck. Whoa! Mac, look out!"

Mac watches the truck barrel right for their car as she swerves in the middle of a busy four-lane road. Thank goodness she doesn't hit anybody as horns blare and tires screech. Her tires included. She saves the vehicle, and the pursuit begins. Mac tells Spencer to call Williams to alert the local authorities. Spencer makes the call while he holds on for dear life.

"Where did you learn to drive? Hold on. He's turning. Oh, great! Another one of these narrow roads." Spencer tries to hold on to the dash with only one good hand to keep himself from going through the windshield.

"You can jump out if you can't handle the way I drive. I'll pick you up on my way back." Mac flashes a grin his way.

"No, no. I'm good. I'm just not used to riding shotgun."

"Well, you are today. So hang on. He's turning again, and I can't see the road sign. They don't name their roads up here. I haven't seen a road sign since we left the main highway."

Seth drives the old Chevy as if his life depends on it. He lets off the gas as he slides into the corners, then he brakes hard to straighten the truck. The brakes begin smoking. There is no way the truck can keep up with that kind of abuse. Mac is on his bumper when he hits a pothole in the road. The truck goes airborne.

Mac screams, "Here we go! Be ready to bail. He can't save this one."

When several seconds pass, Spencer yells back, "He saved it. I should ask him where he learned to drive! He needs to be a race car driver. That is fancy driving."

Mac doesn't even look at him. Yet here she is right on this guy's bumper, and Spencer hasn't commented that she can drive too! Her blood boils. She wants Seth to stop—and now. She is afraid he'll hit another car and cause more bodily harm.

"I'll tap the back of the truck and see if I can spin the truck out," Mac states.

"Just a suggestion, we should wait for help. We are in no position for a pit maneuver. This road is unfamiliar to us, and we don't want to kill ourselves in the process."

"I agree, but he's not slowing. Instead, he's going faster. If he hits another car while I am chasing him, it will devastate me. No more deaths from this guy. It is now or never!"

Spencer senses impending danger. So he picks up his cell phone and hits the speed dial for Williams. Spencer relays their plan when Mac taps the left rear quarter panel of the truck with her vehicle. Both cars skid across the asphalt. The truck hits the soft dirt on the shoulder of the road and begins flipping. Seth hangs partially out of the windshield after the last roll. The truck lands on Seth's legs. Mac runs to the truck, but she senses Seth is beyond help. The EMTs pronounce him dead at the scene.

Mac is glad and sad. Sad, she took a life but pleased this ordeal is over. She is leaning against the car when her dad arrives. She rehashes the events with him and tells him the details.

Myles asks, "Did anyone search the truck for the rifle? It was not in the vehicle in the gorge."

"I didn't," Spencer says as he walks over toward the truck. One of the crime scene techs hands him a pair of latex gloves as he looks into the truck and sees nothing.

Myles yells over, "Check behind the seat!"

Spencer can't get the seat to release. It must have gotten wedged in place during the accident, and he's working with only one good arm. "I can't pull it down with only one arm. Can I get help here?" Spencer pleaded.

A few techs step in to help Spencer. They used a crowbar to get the seat to pull forward. Sure enough, a Remington 223 caliber long gun is there. They clap. Myles suggests Spencer hand it over to the techs. They will transport it to the lab.

Mac looks at her dad and Spencer. "I'm so grateful all of us are safe. I'm sorry Seth is dead, but I am also glad the murders will end. So does anybody want to give a girl a lift back to Atlanta? They impounded my vehicle."

Myles instructs his passengers to climb into the Suburban. George will drive them home. On the way, they discuss the case. Chastain confirms Seth's financials didn't reveal any large deposits or withdrawals over the last year and that Seth was an officer with the Atlanta Police Department. The only thing missing is Drake. No one has seen him since he left the ER earlier in the day. The group calls Williams on speakerphone and gives him a rundown of the action.

Williams advised he left two messages on his voice mail. Maybe he will show up at the office or call Williams back. Mac doesn't like loose ends, and Drake is a loose end.

The next day, back in Atlanta, Mac meets the task force members in the conference room. She wants to thank them for their tremendous job and support during the investigation. Afterward, they placed Mac on paid leave while the results of the internal investigation are pending. She will have to endure questions from Internal Affairs, but Williams tells her she will be fine because she followed protocol even though she couldn't stop Seth's truck. She didn't intentionally cause his death.

"I hope so. I knew no other way to get this guy to stop. After IA questions me, I am taking a week of vacation to try to sort out some things. Is it okay?"

"Yes, as long as you promise you'll return to the job. The job isn't always like this, and I hope you take Spencer with you on vacation. He could use one too!"

"I just might ask if he feels up to a little relaxation on a beach somewhere."

Mac stands from her chair and walks out of the office into the Atlanta heat, pondering her next move with Spencer and what it might hold for her future.

Other Books by A.M. Holloway

Flames of Murder (Mac Morris Thriller Book 2)

Promises of Murder (Sheriff Jada Steele Book 1)

Pieces of Murder (Digger Collins Thriller Book 1)

MOA (Mac Morris Thriller Book 1)

~~~~~~~~~~~~~

Visit www.amholloway.com to sign up for my reader's list and updates

or simply scan the code.

Made in the USA
Monee, IL
06 August 2022

11099182R00118